Praise for *Renovati*

"This is a fine novel about trying to love, trying to forgive, and trying to build something perfect: a trapeze glide from the comic into the tragic and back to a place of balance in between. A pleasure in three sure-handed parts."

—Fred Stenson

"As the title suggests, this book is about making things new —a new life in a new country, a new house in a new city, a new way of life for the son who grows up an artist in a culture that frowns upon art. As Onkel Jacob Sawatsky (a one-man chorus in this novel) might say, "Will you look at that! The boy has put us in an Englisher book!" The "immigrant experience" may never have been told so entertainingly or convincingly as it is in this story of a German Mennonite family adjusting to life in western Canada. The final installment of this story will make you want to read the whole lovely, funny, and sometimes heartbreaking book again, armed with new insight gained from a painful glimpse at the past. While telling the tale of his gradual parting from his Mennonite family, the young narrator portrays his parents and colourful relatives with such love and understanding as to prove a full parting impossible. This is an important story, beautifully told."

—Jack Hodgins

"At first, *Renovating Heaven* lulls the reader into the nostalgic comfort of hilarious family memories, but the accumulated gathering of comic events adds up to a tragic portrait of people displaced by history, stifled by exaggerated belief systems, buoyed up and crushed by faith and love. Andreas Schroeder is a liar and a rascal indeed."

—Armin Wiebe

"I have enjoyed all of Andreas Schroeder's varied and beautifully written books but *Renovating Heaven* will surely remain my favourite. It has the two ingredients for great writing; humour and tragedy. He reveals the secretive fundamentalist Mennonite religious-culture experienced in his boyhood and youth with ruthless clarity. To gain his freedom from its awful rigidity he suffered his Father's rejection. His inner turmoil and his Father's inability to comprehend what was happening are heartrending, and so funny. Schroeder presents this remarkable achievement as a work of fiction. This family portrait, written with love and compassion, is a masterpiece."

—Edith Iglauer

"*Renovating Heaven* is a moving account of growing up with one foot in the traditional Mennonite world and the other in the godless world of the "Englishers." It is humorous, tragic and masterfully written.

—Howard White

"*Renovating Heaven* could as easily have been entitled *A Portrait of the Artist as a Young Mennonite.* Dancing lightly along the boundary between autobiography and fiction, *Renovating Heaven* effortlessly evokes the humour, pain and exhilaration of a young man's emergence from a narrow religious background into the ambiguities and excitement of a writer's life. As his awakened imagination induces him to come to terms with his parents' gnarled inner lives, however, he is forced to contemplate the subtle varieties of sin and evil, and the complex character of his own inheritance—and to become, in a sense, the instrument of the only redemption his parents will ever receive."

—Silver Donald Cameron

"In *Renovating Heaven*, Schroeder writes like Garrison Keillor when Keillor's hot. He's got the American humourist's wonderful knack of combining love with ridicule, and joy with hints of the dark side of family life. This is just a beautiful piece of work."

—Harry Bruce

RENOVATING

HEAVEN

RENOVATING HEAVEN

a novel in triptych
by

Andreas Schroeder

OOLICHAN BOOKS
LANTZVILLE, BRITISH COLUMBIA, CANADA
2008

Library and Archives Canada Cataloguing in Publication

Schroeder, Andreas, 1946-
Renovating heaven / Andreas Schroeder.

ISBN 978-0-88982-248-1

1. Schroeder, Andreas, 1946- —Fiction.
2. Mennonites—Canada—Fiction.

I. Title.

PS8587.C5R45 2008 C813'.54 C2008-903045-1

We gratefully acknowledge the financial support of the Canada Council for the Arts, the British Columbia Arts Council through the BC Ministry of Tourism, Small Business and Culture, and the Government of Canada through the Book Publishing Industry Development Program, for our publishing activities.

Published by
Oolichan Books
P.O. Box 10, Lantzville
British Columbia, Canada
V0R 2H0
Printed in Canada

To my sisters, Angelika and Christine
who were willing to let me remember it
from my perspective;
to my Tante Gertraut, who took in the lost
and the black sheep indiscriminately;
to Elder Wiens who tried his best,
and—most of all—to
my wife Sharon
who has put up with the result
for over three decades

EATING MY FATHER'S ISLAND

one

Letters like the one my father received on September 8, 1956, always caused consternation in our family.

For one thing, the address was typed, not handwritten. For another, the return address—BALLISTER, CLARKE, MARSHALL & ROBSON—was printed in gilt-colored ink. Only "the English" sent letters like that.

Our own mail, hand-scrawled and air-mailed to Agassiz from Mennonite villages in West Prussia, always arrived at rigidly pre-determined times—birthdays, weddings and anniversaries—and always contained the same things: a single-page report, an updated family snap, a Bible verse and a pious exhortation. Letters from the English usually contained very formally typed documents with lots of heretofores and whereases and notwithstandings. Such letters almost always meant trouble.

That evening after milking, Father and I took the letter over to Onkel Jacob Sawatsky. Everybody always took their English letters to Onkel Jacob Sawatsky. Onkel Jacob was a short, fat man with a disproportionately large nose and a receding chin, both of which he'd tried to camouflage with a goatee and spectacles. He was rumored to be on a first-name basis with John Diefenbaker.

Onkel Jacob was publically ostracized but privately admired for his perplexing ability to make sense of heretofores and notwithstandings. His farm was a mess—just a sham of a farm, really—with broken machinery and cast-off junk cluttering the yard in a very un-Mennonite manner. His daughters danced around on his nose, everybody knew that, and his wife spent most of her life in bed. Their garden was always choked with weeds, and their herd records were in total disarray. In fact, most people visited the Sawatskys just to feel better about their own neat farms—and, since they just happened to have them in their pockets, to have their English letters unpuzzled.

Onkel Jacob took Father and me to his "office"—a tiny windowless room off the kitchen that had once been a pantry, barely big enough for Father to sit and me to stand. The long pause that followed, as he gravely examined Father's letter, was probably the main thing Onkel Jacob lived for—those few moments when his social betters in Agassiz's Mennonite community were obliged to acknowledge, however tacitly, his brief supremacy. Then he laid the letter on his desk with the appropriate gravity.

"So you entered a contest," he stated flatly, though not quite neutrally. Coming from any other relative this statement would have been unequivocally accusing. Entering a contest, a worldly contest, an English contest, had to be considered, for a Mennonite, very poor form. Not one of the Seven Deadly Sins, not enough to be mentioned from the pulpit on Sunday morning, but nevertheless an undeniable instance of flawed moral judgment.

Father's face reddened. "I had to get Margarete's sewing machine fixed," he protested.

Even at my age—nine years and ten months—I knew that father's embarrassment was really due to the fact that he'd been unable to fix the machine himself.

"And then he wanted me to fill out a . . . some sort of . . . paper for a contest," Father grumped. "Something about winning an island—I can never understand the English when they jabber so fast. I wanted nothing to do with it, so he said he'd fill it out for me. What did he want with me and a contest, for heaven's sake? I'd already paid him for the repairs."

We all shrugged automatically, in unison. Who could understand the English? We were Fraser Valley farmers, war refugees from West Prussia, working ourselves to the bone to pay off our passage and the mortgage on the farm. The idea of winning an island was so incongruous, so absurd and utterly frivolous, it might as well have come from another planet.

Onkel Jacob frowned and refolded the letter like an Elder presenting the clincher in a scriptural dispute. "Well, but now you have the business," he said in a way that clearly meant: That's what comes from such foolishness. "What has happened now, with this Island In The Sun contest, is that they've had a draw, and the entry they drew was yours. You've won a prize—First Prize, this letter says.

"And First Prize, in this contest, is that island."

two

My father was a pessimist who'd come by his pessimism honestly.

According to Mennonite tradition, the firstborn son inherited the entire estate. The second son became a minister. All daughters and subsequent sons were out of luck. My father was the last offspring of a family of four sons and three daughters, ten years younger than his next-youngest sibling, and an excessively shy, reclusive boy in a loud and rambunctious household. Throughout his youth he invariably found that whenever he finally arrived anywhere, everyone was already packing up and heading somewhere else.

It didn't help that he was also the only member of the Niebuhr clan who refused to worship at the sacred altar of farming—a pursuit specifically and historically designated for the Mennonites by God. He dodged his chores and summer farm-work whenever possible, spending all his time and money on darkroom photography. At age seventeen, rummaging unhappily through the small bag of career options his family had made available to him, he chose—because he assumed it would leave him plenty of time for his darkroom—to apprentice to a cabinet-maker. He was wrong. His master kept him hard at work from morning till night, and considered his photography a counter-productive distraction. The apprentice reports filed under *Reinhard, Youngest* in Elder Niebuhr's filing cabinet—in a drawer that also contained the fertility reports on each of his thirty-five Holstein cows—were terse and unenthusiastic.

In 1944, at the age of twenty-one, Reinhard Niebuhr astonished everyone by managing, after a lengthy courtship that seemed to be going nowhere, to convince the lively and popular Margarete Klassen to marry him. Margarete was the sixth daughter of the Elder Heinrich Klassen, a rich landowner from neighbouring Heuboden County.

Margarete was an accomplished musician and a nursing apprentice. They had met a few years earlier at a Mennonite Youth Camp on St. Christoph's Island, where both had been attending a religious retreat. The lively and artistic Margarete seemed the very opposite of the meticulous, taciturn Reinhard, who spent half his spare time photographing rocks and buildings and the other half printing them again and again, in endless variations of tone and contrast, in his darkroom. Though their talks and walks around St. Christoph's Island had been awkward and inconclusive ("You should try photographing people too, Reinhard," Margarete had urged, and he had complied—producing a series of portraits of a child's teddy-bear), Reinhard had remembered only her eventual promise to see him again in Berlin, where she was completing her apprenticeship. In his recollections over the following years, the island had become for him an increasingly idyllic and symbolic place, and he had returned there often, alone on his bicycle, to retrace their walks and imagine a life with Margarete.

But in 1939 the Second World War had stomped into everyone's life "without even taking its barn boots off" as Elder Niebuhr had put it. When the Nazis eventually rejected the Mennonites' claim of historical Conscientious Objector status, Reinhard was given three months' training as a cook and herded, like thousands of other insufficiently dedicated German soldiers, out to the Russian Front.

In the years that followed, both the Niebuhr and the Klassen clans suffered many casualties. The first wave paralleled Germany's last offensives; the second, its collapse. Sons, fathers and brothers died in uniform; mothers and daughters died when the Russian army over-ran their farms and turned everyone into refugees. Reinhard himself was wounded twice and, during one of his brief medical furloughs, he finally managed to convince Margarete to marry him. He spent his entire accumulated army pay to rent a cabin on St. Christoph's Island for their weekend honeymoon, and much of Saturday afternoon and Sunday morning photographing Margarete on walks and benches all over the island. By Monday noon he was back on a troop train, bound for Poland.

How he survived that slaughter, Reinhard never

confided to anyone but Margarete. His unit was flung at Partisan irregulars in Kracow, chased down through Czechoslovakia by Cossaks, and hounded back west by the rapidly advancing Red Army. He arrived in Germany just in time to be corralled by the occupying Americans, who penned him in a prison camp in Essen and nearly starved him to death.

On his release in 1947 Reinhard took one look at his bombed-out, ruined country, gathered up Margarete and his year-old son Peter, whom he'd only just met—that was me—and applied for emigration to Canada.

But Canada didn't need any nurses or cabinet-makers. The labour market in the West had been decimated by the war, and Canada's farmers were clamouring for cheap farm help. Ruefully, and despite the fact that Margarete was mortally terrified of cows, Reinhard registered them both as farm labourers and joined the throngs of emigrants jostling for position at the docks in Bremerhaven. Once again, he felt as if he was arriving just as everyone else was leaving.

three

Onkel Jacob had promised not to tell anyone and I'd only told my best friend Gerd and his cousin Willy, both of whom had sworn to keep their mouths shut, but within half a day the whole church knew about Father's island. I could tell because of the way all the men on the left and all the women on the right suddenly looked at us that Sunday as we walked up the aisle. Everybody was trying to decide how to react to this bizarre news. To a farming community like Agassiz, owning an island was either totally exotic or utterly silly—insofar as the two weren't the same thing.

"Is it really true?" Tante Waltraut Doerksen burst out right after church—but safely beyond the church steps in the parking lot—"that you're going to give up your farm to go live with the English on an island?" Onkel Fritz, one of the eight Klassen families who lived on Edison Road and always gave their English postman nightmares because every single family had a son or father named John, came up and congratulated Father on "winning Vancouver Island". The Reverend Erich Friesen, in his gentle but firm way, took Father aside in the church foyer and reminded him that help was always available if he was experiencing any undue spiritual turbulence.

We weren't sure ourselves what to make of the news. An island was obviously something the English prized highly—they wouldn't have made it a First Prize otherwise. But if it involved leisure time or vacations, it was decades too early for us. With our mortgages and CPR emigration debts, that was something we couldn't even think about, let alone aspire to. The only holidays the Mennonites ever talked about involved heaven.

Eventually Onkel Jacob offered to drive us out to Britannia Beach in his farm truck. That, according to his further enquiries, was approximately where our island was located. Today you can get to Britannia Beach from Agassiz in less than three hours, hissing comfortably along a modern highway. In 1956 the journey took an entire day, struggling over two mountain passes on a single-lane gravel road, with Onkel Jacob, Mother and Father squeezed into the cab up front and the three kids—my two younger sisters and me—bouncing around on smelly barn blankets in the back. By the time we pulled into the first service station on the outskirts of Baline Bay, eleven hours later, we needed everything they had to offer—gas, air, oil, water, toilet, tire repair and a fan belt.

I don't know how all this was registering up front, but we kids were absolutely goggle-eyed. At first it was just the smell—the mysterious, slightly repulsive briny stench of approaching ocean. Then, a few turns later, the stunning switch from landscape to seascape. All along the left side of the highway, for miles in both directions, was rocky beach and low surf; boats, log pilings, kelp-covered reefs, screeching gulls and an open horizon that seemed to reach to the very edge of the world. My sisters had never seen such a thing.

"You like it?" Onkel Jacob grinned when we stopped at a marina for directions. He waved at the scene as if he were personally responsible for the whole thing. "You must remember this from your passage, Peter. Weren't you already five when your family came over?" He continued right on as if I hadn't nodded. "According to our Citizenship instructor, this is the most island-studded stretch of the B.C. coast."

"We own an island in the middle of . . . all those?" My five-year-old sister Gutrun, almost as tall as I and already in need of spectacles we couldn't afford, was squinting hard at a string of large brush-covered humps dotting the bay about half a mile offshore. In the late-afternoon sun they seemed to hover in the gleaming water like herds of black-backed whales immobilized in one of Father's photographs. Onkel Jacob hoisted his birding-glasses onto his nose.

"Oh I don't know about that. No no; I wouldn't think so. I doubt that anybody would be giving away islands as big as those."

It took us another half hour to find Father's island. The directions said 2.4 miles along Marine Road starting from the B/A station—just past its junction with McDonald Road. I knocked on the cab roof when we passed the gravel road with its sign buried in blackberry bushes, but Onkel Jacob hardly ever paid attention to kids so he had to turn around about a mile later and go back. I knocked on the roof again as we passed the junction a second time, but he didn't stop that time either. When he finally did, after my third, really hard knock, he was a bit peeved.

"What, you think that's McDonald Road?" he complained. "Come on, that's barely more than a cattle trail. So then that . . ." he swung around, scanning the boulder-strewn shore on the other side of the highway . . . "you mean that would be the island?"

I guess I could see his point.

We were looking at a forlorn little pile of rocks about a quarter mile offshore, barely half an acre in size, with just a little fuzz of green on it. Through the birding glasses I made out some salal that I mistook at the time for blueberry bushes, and a lot of bleached driftwood. No beach or obvious landing spots; just rocks and boulders around its entire circumference.

Father and Mother climbed out of the car. "*Na*, have you two mariners found our Paradise already?" Father's forced jauntiness had already taken its cue from our obvious lack of enthusiasm. Mother looked oceanward with a carefully neutral face, shielding her eyes. Onkel Jacob frowned back over his shoulder, pretending to recheck the directions. "Just offshore at the junction of Marine and McDonald," he confirmed. "That looks to be her all right."

Father took the birding glasses and began a slow, methodical scan. Mother and I just looked, not saying anything. But my three-year-old sister Heidi wasn't so careful about hiding her disappointment. "What?" she wailed. "That little thing? It's not even big enough for a heifer!"

"Well we weren't going to farm it, you idiot," I sneered.

"Peter," Mother warned.

Heidi stuck her thumbs in her ears and waggled her fingers at me behind Mother's back.

"Well, did you really think the English were going to give you something for nothing?" Onkel Jacob laughed, an annoyed laugh that showed he hadn't been so sure himself, and now felt embarrassed about his lapse of cynicism. Only Father remained silent, still scanning the island.

"I don't know how we'd ever get onto it anyway," Gutrun grumbled resignedly. "We don't even have a boat." Having inherited a goodly dose of Father's practical nature, she suddenly saw a whole list of problems she'd conveniently ignored before. "And where would we get water to drink anyway? You can't even really land on it; it hasn't got a beach or anything. And in a storm it would probably just go under water."

She climbed back onto the truck's deck and began yanking disconsolately at the scattered pile of barn blankets we'd been sitting on, while I wrestled with the bales that formed the deck's perimeter. Onkel Jacob walked around his truck clockwise and then anticlockwise, examining all his tires and straightening his rear license plate.

"Heidi," Mother warned. "Stay on the road; I don't want you dirtying your school clothes in that ditch." She was wearing her second-best dress with the fancy stitching down the front, and both girls were wearing their good frocks and stockings. Even I'd been convinced to put on my green going-to-town shirt with the snap buttons and the two breast pockets. We'd all wanted to look good in Father's photograph of the family standing proudly in front of its new island.

Finally, Father lowered the birding glasses and handed them off to Mother. He zipped up his jacket and then cleared his throat in a way that I've heard myself do at least a million times since.

"No," he said thoughtfully, rubbing his chin and gazing at the surrounding mountains in a manner already more proprietorial than tourist. "No, I don't think that would happen at all. You can see the high water mark quite clearly on the rocks all around the island."

four

After a supper of bread and borscht, which Mother heated in the kitchenette of a small nearby motel, Father surprised us all by starting to talk about Prussia.

"This stuff was really cheap and easy to come by," he remembered, examining a package of tinfoil drip liners someone had left on the stove. "We used it in our chicken barns back home to make reflectors." He turned it this way and that to catch the light. "For the chicks, right after they were hatched. To keep them warm. And when they called me up for duty in Russia—it was the middle of winter, everybody was freezing to death over there—I sewed whole lengths of it into my coat."

We were nonplussed—for several reasons. First, Father hardly ever talked at length about anything. Second, he virtually never talked about his past—even when we pestered him about it. That's why we were a lot more familiar with Mother's stories, her people, her own West Prussian childhood on the huge Klassen estate, with its many maids and barn-servants, its barns full of fine horses and its more than thirty-five pure-bred Holstein milch cows. To us children it seemed that all our customs, history and heritage came from our mother's side.

"That comes from drowning in Klassens," Father had once grumped. "In Agassiz, if you throw a rock at a Klassen it'll bounce off him and hit two more before it ever hits the ground." In our local Mennonite church, founded in 1951 by my grandfather Heinrich Klassen, every single one of its sixty-one members was related to us on our mother's side. You couldn't find hide nor hair of a Niebuhr anywhere in B.C. All our father's people had settled in Manitoba.

Tonight, over a hundred miles from Agassiz, a circle of tinfoil was all it took to put Father in a reminiscing mood. "Oh *ja*, right in between the shell and the lining. That kept me warmer than anybody could understand. In Moscow, at the Leningrad offensive, I was the only one without frostbite. I even sewed it—laugh if you like—into the lining of my hat."

"Tinfoil?" Onkel Jacob snorted, caught between admiration for ingenuity and a four-centuries-old Mennonite contempt for war and anything associated with it. "Tinfoil!"

Mother laughed. "It's true—when he came back on furlough, he rustled in the most alarming way."

"You sewed it all by yourself, Father?" Gutrun marvelled, never having seen a man anywhere near a sewing machine except to fix it.

"Oh yes, your father was a very accomplished sewer,"

Mother said. "And a photographer, and a carpenter, and . . . so on."

"A cabinet-maker," Father corrected automatically, but let it pass. "Oh *ja,* I had that coat for over a decade, and I'd still be wearing it today if the CPR hadn't lost one of our trunks."

"The CPR," Onkel Jacob snorted, lifting his hand and letting it fall onto the table in resounding agreement. "My God yes, the CPR!"

"I was wearing that coat when I met Margarete on St. Christoph's Island. At our youth camp," Father said, apparently to Onkel Jacob. He seemed to be seeing an entrancing depiction of this on the kitchenette ceiling. "I always felt that God was . . . particularly close to us in those weeks."

"St. Christoph's Island," Onkel Jacob nodded uneasily, unclear where this conversation was going. "*Ja, ja,* St. Christoph's Island."

Mother blushed slightly. "There were always so many gulls," she remembered quickly. "They were very beautiful; great flocks always wheeling and diving."

"Where was I, where was I?" screeched little Heidi, giddy with all this intimate history.

"You didn't appear until we'd been in Canada for almost two years," Mother said fondly, poking her in the stomach.

"And still living in a dirt-floor shack, hoeing corn and beans by hand to pay off our passage," Father groused, though he didn't say it with his usual rancour. "If Edgar Friesen hadn't been so busy counting his profits, he might have saved us that, at very least."

"Oh oh, I believe I smell a whiff of sulphur," laughed

Onkel Jacob, who was distantly related to the Edgar Friesens and thus duty-bound to defend them against all slander. "I'm going to see what I can do about that piece of plywood you wanted. There's still enough light outside so I can scrounge around a bit."

"*Ach* Reinhard, it wasn't true that Edgar was being stingy," Mother said when Onkel Jacob had left, though I was pretty sure she was saying this primarily for our benefit. "It was just that we were the last of our people to arrive. By the time we got here, everybody's credit had been used up."

"Only twenty-five acres," Father grumped, rocking back on his chair's hind legs—something he never did at home. "And there wasn't even enough left over to buy a tractor or machinery."

"Herman and Juergen offered to lend us theirs," Mother pointed out carefully.

"Your brothers live twelve miles away, Margarete," Father said. "They're farming over two hundred acres. When has their machinery ever been available to us?"

"I'm just saying," Mother said.

She sighed and glanced uneasily at us children, all three agog at the frankness of the discussion we were unaccountably being allowed to hear. It wasn't that we weren't aware of these accusations—we'd heard them in bits and pieces for years—but this sudden promotion to temporary adulthood, something that would never have happened at home, felt deliciously risky and unreal.

"Twenty-two acres of grass cut by hand," Father said. "I even had to make my own scythe. The hay had to be turned every twenty-four hours. We pitched from dawn till dusk. Day in, day out. For weeks."

"I know," Mother said. "I was helping you."

"I was helping too," I threw in, taking a chance.

"Under the willow tree, by the slough," Mother agreed. "Every day. Taking care of Gutrun in her cradle."

Gutrun snorted. "I bet you didn't even," she said.

I threw the tinfoil I'd been squashing at her head.

"Totally unfenced land," Father continued. "Seven hundred and nineteen fenceposts, and every one of them dug in by hand."

Now he was talking about something even I remembered clearly. Having to stand under the blazing sun, hour after hour, steadying the posts while Father dug, pounded, stretched wire. The day he'd become so obsessed with his digging and pounding and stretching that he'd stopped listening to me entirely and I'd come home with a spectacular sunburn, my back covered with huge, seeping blisters. Mother had been horrified.

"*Um Himmel's Willen!* How is it possible to abandon a child that's standing less than fifteen inches away from you?!"

Father hadn't answered. He'd looked like he didn't know the answer.

And we still didn't have a tractor. Instead, Father had negotiated an arrangement with the Hoogendoorns on the much larger farm next door, whereby, in exchange for his labour during their major ploughing, seeding and harvesting periods, they extended their operations to include our twenty-five acres. But anything smaller that needed to be done during the rest of the year still had to be done by hand.

We had no car either, nor much hope of getting one. I'd always thought this bothered me more than the rest of the family—the pitying looks from my cousins as they moved over to let us poor church-mice into the back seat on Sunday mornings, where I invariably became car-sick—but it obviously bothered Father too, because he made some remark I didn't catch about "providing work for the Samaritans," which had Heidi shrieking with laughter the way kids do when they're trying to ingratiate themselves over something they don't understand. A sharp look from Mother shut her up.

"They don't mean it, Reinhard," Mother sighed, in a way that gave me my first glimpse of the load of sorrow she carried all her adult life. "They don't mean it, and you know that."

"They may not mean it, but they do it," Father shrugged, almost complacent now because he was winning the argument. "They do it, and they've done it from the day that you and I met. I've never been good enough to marry a Klassen, and they've never missed a chance to make sure I got that message. Deny that, if you can."

Mother didn't say anything for quite a while.

When Onkel Jacob returned, he knocked, but came in right away. He was carrying a fat black marker and a large piece of plywood nailed to a long piece of two-by-four. "You'll have to sharpen the end somehow," he said, dropping the sign by the door. "Here Peter, you write the words on it in really big letters. All capitals, and then fill them in with black. 'No Trespassing'. Can you remember that? D'you want me to write it down for you? 'No Trespassing'."

"The motel owner said he'd lend us his rowboat," Father said. "He said the water's calmest between six and nine."

At eight o'clock they set out for the island, now sharply silhouetted by the setting sun. I'd finished the sign as per instructions—*No Trespissing*—and Father had whittled the stud to a sharp point. Onkel Jacob studied the sign, grinned briefly and stowed it in the bottom of the boat. Father climbed in awkwardly, got a good grip on the gunwales and let Onkel Jacob do the rowing. Pretty soon I could only tell who was who by Onkel Jacob's big straw hat. I watched them through the birding glasses as they arrived at the island, rowing in and pushing off several times before they found a place to land. Eventually, Onkel Jacob climbed onto the rocks and dragged the sign to the island's only knoll. I saw him pounding it in with a large rock, leaving it standing at a slight angle.

He returned to the boat, but for some reason they didn't push off. Then I saw that Father was going to photograph the sign. He never photographed anything freehand, and it took him a long time to clamber out of the boat, find a level spot and set up his tripod. When the camera was ready he crouched down behind it, but almost immediately stood back up again. Climbing carefully to the sign, he pulled at it until it stood perfectly straight, checked it from several angles, then pounded it more firmly into the knoll.

Then he returned to the camera and snapped the picture.

five

It took a while for the true impact of Father's island to register on our lives—and that was largely because two conflicting assessments of its value began to circulate.

The first, probably originating with Onkel Jacob, held that the whole thing had turned out to be a low trick—exactly what you'd expect from the English. Father's island was just a worthless heap of rocks and bush.

The second, definitely originating with Onkel Jacob, resulted from his later conversation with Agassiz's only banker, Mr. Richmond Elliott Tunbridge.

Being manager of the Bank of Montreal, which held our mortgage, Mr. Tunbridge was most intrigued to hear of Father's island. It wasn't long before he'd informed himself about all its particulars. His eventual assessment, mentioned in confidence to Onkel Jacob, differed considerably from Onkel Jacob's initial impression. Mr. Tunbridge felt that while the island might not have a great deal of value just at present, it was bound to gain substantially from the extension of power and population into the Squamish Valley, which was expected to happen within the next decade or two. He saw it, therefore, as a "significant long-term investment".

Since Mr. Tunbridge was undeniably English, his grasp of financial matters could hardly be denied. Thus the following conclusion evolved: The Canada Sewing Machine Company had tried to pass off onto Father what they considered a worthless pile of rocks and bush. But the joke had been on them. They hadn't counted on Mr. Tunbridge and urban development. Result: Mennonites l, The English 0.

Being a pessimist, Father knew that safety lay more reliably in assessment number one, and I believe he truly tried to hold to that interpretation—especially since it provided him with fewer problems within the Mennonite community. In time, however, there were signs that he hadn't been able to keep at least trace amounts of assessment number two from seeping into his subconscious.

As befitted a man who had always kept his emotional life on a painfully short leash, these signs appeared initially as the subtlest of diminutions: a little less brooding, a little less bitterness, less tightfistedness. In time: a tiny bit more tolerance, more equanimity, even a trace of hope. I stumbled on dramatic evidence of the latter on the rainy Sunday afternoon following the delivery of the official land deed—in the hands of a photographer who'd insisted on photographing our entire family gathered around the sewing machine—when I heard a voice that sounded both like and unlike

Mother murmuring something behind the closed door of our living room. My thoughtless bursting in sent Mother scrambling hastily off Father's lap, her hair and composure in considerable disarray. "*Na was?*" Father protested, trying vainly to keep Mother from fleeing. "Just look at him, he's more embarrassed than we are; hey, come on, we're married, for heaven sakes!"

In church too, Father greeted people less diffidently, stood and sat more confidently, and during the latter part of the sermon, when he normally became fidgety, I saw him wide awake and preoccupied, scribbling busily into the margins of his church bulletin. They were just numbers—I snuck a look—but the upshot was that several days later, after another discreet and confidential conference with Onkel Jacob, the whole community—including Jacques Lafreniere, proprietor of Honest Ron's Auto and Tractor Emporium, the only used-car dealership in Agassiz—knew that Father was seriously considering buying a car.

This was news to Father, who had merely been exploring the possibility of installing a used car engine into a burned-out Massey Harris chassis he'd found jettisoned at the town dump. But the prompt and unctuous visit by Lafreniere, with hastily borrowed Bible poking out of his jacket pocket, turned this unlikely idea in a more productive direction. In his eagerness to convince Father of the many virtues of a rusty 1936 Chevrolet Town Sedan, Lafreniere said: "She might not be so fast, she, and she might not be so pretty, *bon,* and hokay, de back seat she is missing and de back window she is gone, but *sacrement* and *Mere de Christ*, she is so solid-built, dat one, she could *probablement* tow a barn!

"Tow?" Father asked, turning to me. "What means "tow"?"

"*Ziehen,*" I explained. "Pulling."

"*Halage,*" Lafreniere encouraged, sensing an opening. "Drag. Haul. Hey, I even trow in a old trailer hitch."

"Why for do I want to pull my barn?" Father asked Lafreniere, genuinely puzzled.

"I'm not saying you want, *helas;* I'm just saying you could," Lafreniere explained, which somehow didn't clarify anything and undoubtedly became yet another entry in Father's growing file on the weirdness of the English—even when they were French.

But an idea had taken root, and while Lafreniere went home disappointed, Father was oddly thoughtful for several days, secretive for a few more, and triumphant for a night (during which he and Mother talked until midnight). Then, on the first available rainy day, Father walked all the way over to Onkel Jacob's farm, they both called on Mr. Richard Elliott Tunbridge, and an hour later Father bought the old sedan off Lafreniere's lot for two hundred dollars, at twenty-five dollars down and five dollars a month—trailer hitch included.

According to Onkel Jacob, who was still shaking his head several weeks later, Father spent the largest part of his negotiations at the car lot lamenting the missing back seat, the missing back window, and the excessive amount of chrome on the Chevrolet's bumpers—an excrescence self-evidently offensive to God, the Church and every right-thinking Christian. Lafreniere had finally solved this problem by dropping the price of the car by fifty dollars and throwing in a can of black stove paint. "But you'll 'ave to paint 'er couple times a year eh?" he warned. "Because dat chrome dere, she won't take de paint so good."

For the next few days Father hauled in all the horse-drawn farm equipment he'd been promised for nothing by nearby farmers, and modified the hitches to fit the old sedan. He salvaged a set of winter chains from the garbage dump, and, with these chains fitted to the sedan's back wheels for more tractor-like traction, we were ready and champing at the bit for the spring.

Incongruously hitched to a horse-mower, an ancient swather, a steel-wheeled hay wagon or even an antique six-gang plough, the once-elegant Town Sedan churned and skidded through our fields like a Marxist demonstration of the class struggle, its acres of chrome shining defiantly through thick layers of mud and rust. Father drove, while I stood in the place of the conveniently missing back seat, my head sticking out through the conveniently missing back window, frantically pulling and pushing on the long levers as per Father's shouted instructions.

It took me a while to get the hang of it, and even then I could only move the heavier teamster's levers with a mixture of panic and desperation, but with practice and more axle grease, we managed. "Getting better," Father acknowledged after we'd mowed our first five-acre patch in the field closest to the house, from which Mother and the girls had waved and shouted continuously for the first half hour. "Try to set the cutter down a little earlier when we swing around in the corners."

I glowed at the way he'd said 'we'.

To everyone's amazement, the system actually worked. The car was virtually indestructible, and the farm machinery simple and solidly built. Parts, if needed, were always available in the weeds behind the manure piles of practically every farm in the Fraser Valley.

And on Sundays, for the drive to church in our very own car, I washed off the mud, pulled off the chains, and shoved in the wooden bench that Father had built. A bench that had been painted—it goes without saying—with black stove paint.

six

We didn't visit Father's island for quite a while after that. There was really no need—we were already getting maximum value from its mere existence. Father, now a "farmer, car-owner and island-proprietor," had never been so happy or so optimistic.

Well, "happy" was perhaps an exaggeration. I think Father was congenitally incapable of unconstrained happiness. But in a suppressed, pessimistic sort of way he was learning to allow himself tiny slippages of pleasure, small mistakes of illicit contentment. He seemed to be learning, slowly and in anxious, guilty increments, to cut himself a bit of slack.

On one occasion, having finished a field at 3 pm, he actually chatted in the kitchen with Mother for over half an hour before heading back out. Mother was so startled, she kept waiting for the other shoe to drop—but that was it, it was the second shoe; she'd simply missed the dropping of the first.

On another occasion, coming back from town at suppertime, Father waltzed into the house with a small package of half-melted ice cream, admittedly only large enough for Mother and us kids—he still couldn't treat himself with a clear conscience—but he looked quite pleased with the delighted uproar he caused.

Our farm, too, was buoyed up by Father's island. That spring we planted several acres of raspberries for summer cash flow, invested that cash in three thousand chickens to tide us over the winter when the cows produced less milk, and added a brace of pigs to recycle the farm's compost and slop.

At the end of the summer, as a reward for everyone's dawn-till-dusk labours, Father drove us down to Harrison Hot Springs "where all the English waste their money." We spread our blankets on a far corner of the Harrison Hotel's luxurious lawns, unwrapped our provisions, and then we wasted money with the best of them: a whole Popsicle for each kid—both halves—and two bottles of Kik Cola to go with Mother's homemade bread, homegrown tomatoes and potato salad.

After the meal, Mother lay back on a blanket and divided her time between watching the English parading around with their liveried entourages, and reading a book she'd been trying to finish ever since we'd arrived in Canada. We kids had a great time chasing dragonflies and playing an impromptu game of dodge-ball with a tightly tied-up blanket. The blanket-ball was so huge that it flattened little Heidi whenever it bopped her, and her lusty belly-laugh each time she was knocked down soon had everyone in stitches—even Father, who, after concocting our ball, had settled down to fixing the broken kitchen clock he'd brought along "just to have a look inside".

We'd so rarely heard Father laugh that each time it happened, the two astounded kids without the ball invariably became perfect targets for the kid with it, so the game never stopped. By the time a splendidly uniformed hotel doorman came over and told us we weren't allowed to picnic on hotel property, we were mostly exhausted anyway.

Just because we found no time to visit Father's island, however, didn't stop Father from hatching plans for it. He wouldn't tell us what those plans were, but it was a safe bet there was a direct relationship between the sketches he was making in church and the growing heap of salvage behind our manure pile. I guessed that the collection of old railway ties he'd picked up from an abandoned CPR right-of-way were intended for a dock, and the buckets of rusty bolts soaking in old engine oil were intended for its assembly. It was less clear what a large collection of old bedsprings from the municipal dump might be for, and I couldn't make any sense whatever of the thirty-seven car wheels he'd acquired from the same place. There were door and window frames from a nearby house abandoned after the 1948 flood, and enough old water pipes to span the ocean floor from the mainland to the island. There was even a broken porcelain toilet—when we didn't even have an inside toilet ourselves.

The first indication that Father's plans were outgrowing the limits of his own daydreams came one wet and unusually cold morning in October. Steam rose faintly from every flank and nostril in our barn, as we hunched under our cows, milking.

"Listen Peter; you have a library card, right?"

I froze. This was a loaded question. My parents didn't approve of ungodly books, and that's about the only kind the English library in Agassiz had to offer. I'd had no choice but to forge Father's signature to a library card application, and I always hid my library books in the hayloft.

"It's because I've been finding English library books in the hayloft," Father said neutrally, expertly redirecting a teatful of milk into the open mouth of one of our thirty-odd barn cats. For the next few minutes, the sound of unusually large streams of milk bellowing into my milk pail covered my confusion.

"Well okay, never mind, we'll let that pass. What I wanted to ask you—do you think they'd have a book, the English, about boats?"

"I guess they might," I quavered, still not quite sure I'd slipped through the noose on this one.

"You bring it home and let me have a look at it."

At the Agassiz Public Library, during school lunch hour, I asked the librarian for a book on boats. Lunch Period was short, the school was three blocks away, and I didn't have much time. I took the first book she offered and pelted out the door.

"*Jane's Fighting Ships?*" Father puzzled, slowly sounding out the title. "So now the English have a woman running their navy?" I had a quick look at some of the pictures and diagrams of hundreds of corvettes, minesweepers and aircraft carriers. "This is probably not exactly what you had in mind," I apologized.

"Well, a boat's a boat," Father shrugged. "But we'll have to modify the lines a bit, I can see that."

Which was how we discovered that Father was going to build a boat.

seven

For the next several weeks, after the milking and barn-cleaning and calf-feeding and chicken-feeding and pig-feeding and wood-chopping were done, Father and I struggled with the design of his boat.

"It's got to be pointy at one end, Father. That's how you know you're going forward."

"There are boats without points," Father said, gesturing at the aircraft carrier *Midway*. "The thing is, you could load a lot of building materials on a boat like that."

"But it looks dumb, Father."

"So does our car," Father said. "But it gets our hay baled, doesn't it?"

Father started work on his barge a few months later.

His construction methods, adapted entirely from his cabinet-making experience, resolutely ignored three thousand years of boatbuilding history, from the Phoenicians to the English. He saw the ocean as an invader that had to be repelled with unequivocal strength and rigidity. To accomplish this, he butt-glued where boat builders caulked, and angled where they curved.

He had to build his barge in the hayloft because there was no other covered area available that would let him assemble a fifteen- by ten-foot vessel and still get it out the door. All its constituent materials were salvaged from the municipal dump and the nearby house that had been abandoned after the '48 flood.

The result, according to Onkel Jacob, looked like "a hay wagon with a hard-on," presumably in reference to the eight-foot tall two-by-four sailing mast Father had installed as auxiliary propulsion. The whole thing was so heavy that when the time came to haul it out of the hayloft, four men tugging in unison couldn't lift it an inch.

"Use the bale-claw tackle," our neighbour, Jake Hoogendoorn, suggested. "If it can raise eight bales hauling in, it oughta be able to lower a barge hauling out."

They chained the barge to the bale-claw and hitched the haul-back line to the back of our car. I was delegated to drive because everybody else wanted to watch this from a good vantage point. As the line tightened and the barge rose off its chocks, the barn's timbers groaned and the tackle sang like an over-stretched violin string. "Easy there, easy now!" Father urged, watching the tackle anxiously and looking like he was reciting the Lord's Prayer. He was talking more to the barge than to me. "Easy now. Easy does it."

The barge emerged unsteadily through the hayloft's

double doors and sailed slowly along the hay-boom toward the tip of the roof peak. In addition to her forward motion, she was oscillating slightly, dipping and swaying. When she hit the trip mechanism that changed her direction from horizontal to vertical, a loud crack from the take-up pulleys sent an alarming tremor through the entire rigging.

Everybody tensed. I stopped the car. The men looked at each other questioningly, and then they all looked at Jake Hoogendoorn. Jake shrugged. "I dunno," he said. "Maybe too hard on the linkage. No choice but to keep on going, though."

At this point Mother headed back into the house, saying she couldn't bear to watch anymore.

Father took a deep breath and told me to start up again. I did. The barge continued to descend, pulleys squealing and linkages screeching. Suddenly it began to pick up speed. "Slow down!" Father hollered, panic in his voice. "Slow down the car!"

But I couldn't slow down the car. I was already braking with all my might. All four wheels were locked up tight, and the car was being dragged bodily across the barnyard.

"Holy shit!" Onkel Jacob yelled. "Throw in some bales!"

Each man grabbed a bale and hurled it under the barge. As her descent quickened, they had just enough time to fling in one more bale each. The barge slammed down on the bales in an explosion of hay and hay-dust, flattening them into mats. But they'd cushioned her fall, and when the dust settled, she hadn't suffered any significant damage.

"Solid," Father congratulated himself as if he'd never had any doubt. "She's totally solid. It'll take a typhoon to sink this boat."

The first time we shoved the *John 3:16* ("The most widely-read verse in the Bible," Father explained) into our hayfield slough, she went down like a lead ingot. But another eighteen inches of freeboard and three more gallons of roofing tar seemed to end her submarine tendencies. After that, she floated—"wallowed" according to Onkel Jacob—and Father was able to add the cosmetics like a rudder and oarlocks. He scheduled her launch and sea-trials for the following summer.

eight

We were all shocked when we saw Father's island for the second time.

"Ho-lee!" little Heidi exclaimed—an expression she'd just picked up at English school and was now looking for every possible opportunity to use.

"Heidi!" Mother warned sharply.

"Well it's true," Gutrun agreed. "It looks like a play island from here."

The rest of us stared wordlessly at the unimpressive little pile of rocks in the ocean.

Like the slow inexorable process by which coral islands accrete, Father's island had obviously been gaining mass in our minds. In the intervening years it had become at least the size of its name: an island. Father's Island. We'd all begun to use the word recklessly.

Father had been just as vulnerable to this process as the rest of us. Soon after the beginning of his boat project, he'd begun to make offhand remarks about "a little outhouse" for the island. In time it had become a shack, "a small shack". Lately it had been "the cottage". When I looked over at him I saw, for a fleeting moment, a trace of the look I remembered so vividly from earlier years, a hounded, hopeless expression that had always overwhelmed me with feelings of irrational guilt. It did so again as we stood there trying to adjust our sense of proportion, nobody saying anything until we'd gotten a hint of how Father was handling the disappointment.

"You know, it really is a lot farther out to sea than I remembered," he sighed. "I'm going to have to find a lot more pipe than I thought." He paused for a moment, sucking his teeth reflectively. "Well, it's not going to come any closer from being stared at. Let's go move the boat onto the beach."

It took us most of the day to lever and log-roll the *John 3:16* off Onkel Jacob's truck and into the water. Fortunately it was calm—dead calm—with absolutely no wind. When we finally got her in, the *John 3:16* sat in the water like a dock.

"Marvellous," Father beamed. "Better than I'd hoped. She's stable as a barn."

"It's because there's no wind, Father," I pointed out. "No waves either. She won't move fast enough to steer."

"She'll move," Father assured me. "Push her out a bit farther."

I pushed with all my might, and the *John 3:16* floated forward a few yards. When I stopped pushing, she stopped moving.

We stood there waiting for a while, me up to my waist in the water, Father enjoying all that stability from onboard. The boat seemed motionless, although after a while I noticed that she had drifted slightly back toward shore.

"Give another push," Father instructed. "The sail will catch the wind once we're just a bit farther out."

I pushed some more. Harder. Really hard. The boat moved a few more yards, sluggishly.

"Tell you what," Father said. "You push us out into shoulder-deep water, then jump in. We'll just row to the island."

It took me about five minutes to effect that maneuver. When I flopped over the gunwale, the boat barely dipped. We started to row.

"That's it," Father urged. "That's doing it. Row harder; it takes an extra effort at the beginning."

It took an extra effort after the beginning too. We rowed like madmen for about fifteen minutes. We produced a lot of froth and a lot of wave action. What we didn't produce was a lot of progress.

"Okay, rest time," Father gasped. "We're a bit farther out now; maybe we'll catch some wind."

But we didn't.

"What we need is a tow," I suggested, and began waving my wet shirt energetically at a powerboat several miles to the south.

"Stop it," Father said. "Put that shirt down. What if that's a police boat or the Coast Guard? They'd probably make us buy all kinds of permits and licenses."

"But what'll we do?" I said. "We're not getting anywhere this way."

"That's true," Father agreed, after some moments.

I made sure he couldn't see my face before I grinned.

We sat there unmoving for another half hour, waiting for something to change. Seagulls flew curious approach patterns over our heads, trying to hit the *John 3:16* with their droppings. The muted sound of surf drifted over from some high cliffs to the west, and various fish boats and freighters churned their way past at a considerable distance to the east. The sky was clear all the way back to a range of high peaks to the north — the Lions, according to a road map I'd consulted on the way here. It was actually quite beautiful and peaceful, in an unproductive sort of way.

"Well alright," Father said finally, sucking his teeth again. "Let's row back and try again tomorrow. Maybe tomorrow there'll be a bit more wind to work with."

The next day the weather turned, and we woke to a blustery offshore wind. "Just what we need," I rejoiced, sticking a wetted finger into the air. Father looked at the whitecaps dubiously. "A bit more than I had in mind," he said. The *John 3:16* was tugging at her lines with an eagerness he found alarming. We piled in all the freight—mostly used lumber, railway ties and tools—and cast off. This time the boat didn't even need a push. As soon as the sail was up we were off, plunging and bucking through the waves.

It wasn't long before my exhilaration vanished, and Father's alarm increased to full blown consternation. The *John 3:16* was definitely no sailor. She rolled and dove and plunged like a drunken pig. She was so heavy, she couldn't seem to ride up the side of a wave fast enough to avoid being overwhelmed by its crest.

In no time we were shipping water, and Father had to abandon the tiller to bail. I tore down the sail and bailed too. Wave after wave crashed over the gunwales. We were half full of water and losing the race when a passing gill-netter saw our dilemma and stopped to toss us a rope. When Father pointed to his island, indicating where we wanted to be towed, the man on the gill-netter's aft deck shook his head forcefully and towed us right back to the beach. "Don't even think about it!" he hollered as he headed back on his former course. "Not until you've got something that's seaworthy!"

I had to jump out of the *John 3:16* and swim ashore to get the bow-line secured before the wind pushed her back out again. I tied the rope to the nearest log and staggered back to help Father. His face was white and drawn, and he was retching heavily. I was feeling pretty sick myself.

That evening, after Father had fallen into a coma-like sleep which lasted for almost thirteen hours, Mother told me about Father's seasickness during our Atlantic crossing. "He threw up from the day we left Germany until the day we landed in Montreal," she said, shaking her head. "He didn't eat a scrap of food for three weeks. It was all I could do to make him drink some milk every day."

"I just throw up in cars," little Heidi announced. "And when I eat moth bulbs."

"Mothballs," I said, yanking at the ribbon on one of her long braids. "You thought they were candies, didn't you?"

"The Niebuhrs are famous for their delicate stomachs," Mother sighed. "They throw up at the drop of a hat. In wagons, carriages, cars, boats, and airplanes. I find this whole boat-building business incomprehensible."

nine

After our abortive sea-trials with the *John 3:16* we postponed sailing her to Father's island indefinitely.

Instead, Father took to spending his few leisure hours designing and building a brace of "stabilizers" for her. "The man said she wasn't seaworthy," he explained. "And I have to agree. She was jumping around out there like a bucking heifer."

The stabilizers—rectangular float boxes designed to be bolted to both gunwales—were so huge, Onkel Jacob said they made the boat between them look like a baby's head "stuck between Tante Johanna's bazoomas". I don't know where Father got the idea that they were going to reduce the pitching and yawing. It seemed to me just as likely that they'd magnify the wave action. But Father wouldn't hear of it. "It's like life-jackets," he insisted. "It's basically like putting a life-jacket on a boat."

I was impressed at how quickly he'd recovered from our sea-trials. It was as if this little failure had simply pushed him back onto springs which now bounced him even farther forward than he'd been before. He began talking openly about building a summer cottage on his island. He consulted Onkel Werner Klassen, a professional carpenter, about cantilevered construction methods. He spent the last half of Reverend Friesen's Sunday sermons—when the Reverend was just repeating himself anyway—sketching floating bridges with supports that looked a lot like the *John 3:16*, devices for the laying of submarine cable, and a wooden tunnel designed to sit on the ocean floor.

He bought a map of Howe Sound at the Government Office and hung it up in our living room, with a large red dot just north of Horseshoe Bay.

Now a farmer, car-owner, island-owner and a boat-owner, Father's social star was on the rise.

Nobody in Agassiz in the 1950's owned a boat.

Father began receiving transparent hints. "Is it true you're giving tours of your island on a ship?" Tante Doerksen demanded, even before she'd reached the bottom of the church's front steps. "We're really partial to sea cruises, my Willy and I."

The church Executive Committee offered Father a seat on its Fundraising Committee. The Committee's chairman, Walter Klassen, thought an island-and-boat owner would probably have new ideas more or less automatically.

"They seem to think it comes with the territory," Onkel Jacob explained.

Mother, who had consulted Romans 3:6, urged Father to accept. "You work too hard," she pointed out. "You should be able to sit down too, once in a while."

And little Heidi listened carefully but wasn't sure she quite understood. "Are they going to let you play with them, Father?" she asked.

ten

Our first inkling of trouble came on a February morning, when I called the cows in for milking and they wouldn't come.

It's not unusual for one or two cows to loiter during milking call. But on this particular morning, the entire herd stood crowded into a far corner of the field and no amount of calling could attract their attention. I'd only seen cows that distracted during a birth, if a pregnant cow hadn't been removed from the herd in time. Onlooking cows get really frenzied during a birth, and have to be kept well away from the newborn calf.

Some of our cows were pregnant, but none was close enough to term to separate from the herd. This had to be something else.

It wasn't, though. When I got closer I could see a cow in the middle of the huddle, lying prone in a way they only lie after calving. And when I'd chased away the rest of the herd, I found a newborn calf, trampled to death and already flyblown. It must have been born the previous day, or even earlier. We'd only opened this field to our cows the night before, which led me to conclude that the prone cow wasn't one of ours. Half an hour later I found the hole in the fence through which she'd escaped from the Hoogendoorn farm. When I called the Hoogendoorns, they couldn't understand how they'd missed that hole. They'd been looking for their cow for two days.

We milked our cows two hours late that morning, and the Hoogendoorns came over with their truck to haul their cow and dead calf away. Neither they nor we had the slightest inkling how much havoc this incident would eventually cause.

It took a while to become clear. The first cow on our pregnancy schedule was due nine weeks later. A month before her term, she spontaneously aborted.

The next cow gave birth to a stillborn.

So did the next.

When we mentioned this to the Hoogendoorns, they told us they'd been having the same experience.

The hastily summoned veterinarian, normally a loud, cheerful man, didn't have a joke for anyone this time. He blood-tested our entire herd, and the Hoogendoorn's too, and then sequestered himself with both men in the Hoogendoorn's living room. When they emerged, looking ashen, he left quickly without saying goodbye.

Both herds, it appeared, had brucellosis. Brucellosis is a highly contagious disease that causes affected cows to abort their fetuses, effectively rendering them barren. It is also transmittable to humans.

According to Department of Agriculture regulations, both herds had to be destroyed at once.

Two days later, Jake Hoogendoorn drove into our back pasture with his backhoe and dug a huge pit. Then he dug another in his own adjoining field. At that point, Mother took us children to spend the day with our Aunt Hildegard in Rosedale, while Mrs. Hoogendoorn took her brood to her brother's place in Harrison. When we returned, both herds—fifty-six cows, twelve heifers and fourteen calves—had been shot and buried under layers of lime.

I remember walking around our suddenly empty barn in amazement, trying to come to grips with such a stunning turn of events. It was beyond all comprehension. I don't think anyone even cried. Gutrun just sat in the kitchen wide-eyed, watching the world in fear and awe. For once even little Heidi was struck dumb.

As for me, it was beginning to dawn on me that adults weren't really as powerful as I'd thought—nor as much in control of the world. That fact was even scarier than a lot of shot cows. The treasonous, self-protective thoughts that began to push their way up from my subconscious, after so many years of womb-like security in the Mennonite fold, left me breathless with dismay and excitement.

One gauge of how much trouble we were in was the abrupt change in the way my parents prayed. Prayer, especially public prayer in our church, had always been constructed of discreet euphemisms and religious code. An outbreak of youthful rebellion on a Saturday night—a group of Mennonite teenagers caught furtively roller skating at an English roller-rink, say—would be brought to the Lord's attention the next morning as "the strong temptations of the world to which some of our young people have recently fallen prey." Everyone knew precisely who and what was meant, and so, presumably, did God.

But at our supper table the night after our cows had been destroyed, Father suddenly spoke to God with a frightening frankness. "We know, oh Lord, that Your ways are unfathomable to us, Your children, and we know that You always have our best interests at heart.

"But Lord, we've already lost everything once. We lost our farms, our homes and our loved ones in the Great War. We had to abandon our homeland and cross the great ocean to start again in the wilds of a foreign country, and it was hard, Lord; we were only able to do it with Your help.

"Don't deny us Your help this time, Lord.

"Because if You won't help us, we're going to lose everything a second time."

eleven

God's answer to Father's prayer was unexpected and complicated.

Father told us the details after he came home from his appointment with Mr. Richmond Elliott Tunbridge.

We'd all been dreading his meeting with our English banker.

Mr. Tunbridge, Father said, had welcomed him with condolences and much gravity. The destruction of our herd, according to the bank's calculations, had indeed reduced our farm's worth by almost half its original mortgage value, and that, according to strict bank regulations—which even a bank manager had no authority to override—normally triggered the calling-in of the outstanding loan.

But, while not wishing to underestimate the seriousness of the situation, Mr. Tunbridge had nevertheless offered the opinion that all was not lost.

There was, after all, Father's island.

He had taken the liberty—under these extraordinary circumstances, he'd assumed Father would have no objections—of enquiring into the island's current value. A substantial amount of time, after all, had passed since its acquisition, and the Vancouver-Squamish corridor had seen considerable growth.

He had been, he informed Father, pleasantly surprised at what he'd heard. Nothing could be definitively concluded until an official valuation had been undertaken, but the latest forecasts sounded most promising. Moreover, the area's growth showed no signs of slackening.

"So what he said, our Mr. Tunbridge," Father concluded, "was that, once they'd done a proper valuation, if everything came out the way he thought, he'd be prepared to increase our mortgage by two thousand five hundred dollars."

"Two hundred five thousand!" squealed Heidi, bouncing up and down. "Ho-lee!"

"Heidi!" Mother said sharply.

"Two thousand five hundred," Father said, only half frowning. "That would buy us, I asked your brother Walter about this, about half a dozen milk cows and maybe two or three heifers."

"About half of what we had," Gutrun said very seriously. She had decided to be a farmer's wife when she grew up.

"Even a little less," Father agreed. "We'd have to start from scratch with the calves."

"Did you agree to it?" Mother asked carefully.

"I said he could go ahead with the valuation," Father said. "He offered to do that for free."

✻

Reaction in the community was largely positive. "Half a dozen cows for some rocks you can't even farm?" marveled Deacon Jake Goertzen, who questioned Father about it on the following Sunday—but not until they were in the church basement. "I'd grab it before they change their minds."

"A heaven-sent second chance, Brother Niebuhr," enthused John Hildebrand, our old church janitor who still farmed a two-acre plot with one cow. "Because when The Saviour comes—and we know it won't be long now—you'll still be a farmer, so you'll still be able to get into heaven."

Tante Waltraut Doerksen was astounded all over again. "Is this true what I hear?" she burst out—but not until she'd reached our church's front steps—"that the Englishers are going to give you a new herd to farm on your sewing-machine island?"

There were opposing voices, and one of them was Onkel Jacob. "If that's what the English are willing to lend you against that island, it's probably worth five times that much," he pointed out, slurping his milk-porridge in his little office while Father sat and I stood. "My advice: sell the island outright and buy yourself a proper-sized herd." He scrutinized Father's unhappy expression and shrugged impatiently. "You can't run that farm on half a dozen cows, Reinhard. Just not enough cash flow."

It was a worry that Mother—who normally kept her opinions on financial matters to herself—also mentioned. "A bigger mortgage means bigger payments to the bank, Reinhard," she said carefully, that night after supper. "And then there's the car payments. With a smaller herd, where's all that money going to come from?"

Father answered that question three days later, after mysteriously heading toward town on a perfectly workable Tuesday afternoon. "I got it," he said simply when he got back just in time for supper. "In the kitchen at the Harrison Hot Springs Hotel. On the afternoon shift."

Mother was properly startled. "You're going to cook for the English at the Hot Springs?"

"Just assistant cook," Father said, looking sheepish. "Actually, I'll be spending most of my shifts washing pots and pans in the basement. They pay a dollar an hour, but they include meals with that. And I get to take home any leftovers."

Mother's eyes softened, and she gave Father a gentle hug. "I had no idea that island means so much to you," she said.

But a moment later she stiffened abruptly. "Afternoon shift?" she called after Father, who was heading back out to the barn. "What do you mean, afternoon shift? Then who's going to milk our cows?"

twelve

That was the beginning of what surely became the oddest dairy operation in the history of the Fraser Valley.

To accommodate his shift at the Harrison Hot Springs Hotel, Father re-scheduled farming's most basic and ancient ritual, around which every farming community's social, commercial and religious events revolve: early-morning and early-evening milking. It was a move, in farming terms, as radical as changing the times for sun-up and sun-down.

And Father didn't merely fiddle with this schedule. He turned it completely on its head.

At six o'clock every evening, while the rest of the valley's almost thirty thousand cows were being milked in the valley's six hundred and eighty-four barns, our six new cows stood idly at the pasture gate, flicking at flies while Father attacked mountains of pots at the Harrison Hotel. Then at midnight, when Father's shift ended and the valley's thirty thousand cows were lying in their pastures asleep or passing digesting grass from one stomach to another, Father woke me and our dog and we rousted our cows to be milked from 12:30 to 1:30, in the middle of the night.

At six o'clock every morning, when the valley's farmers and cows met once again for their milking appointments, our cows, from habit, ambled over to the pasture gate and just stood there, puzzled at the silence and inactivity. Though Father was up by 7am, he didn't round up the cows until noon, when the barn was hot and the cows inclined to siestas. His rationale was that cows needed to have at least twelve hours between milkings, and since the midnight milking was unavoidable, a noontime milking—which took twice as long because he was on his own at that time of day—was inevitable.

The logic of all this may eventually have made a reluctant sort of sense to the rest of our family, but it completely escaped our cows. Milk production plunged, bovine cooperation deteriorated—much frustrated kicking and bucking—and we began to experience problems with milk let-down.

"Oh, they'll get used to it," Father assured us. "It'll probably take a while, cows are slow about this sort of thing, I've noticed that about chickens too, but they'll get used to it. You'll see."

We tried it Father's way for the better part of six months, but the cows didn't get used to it. They stuck resolutely to the old schedule, eating at the old times and sleeping at the old times. Milking, once a natural part of their day's rhythm and order, now became an interruption, a nuisance. By the end of the summer, we'd even had several cases of milk fever.

Deacon Goertzen professed himself unsurprised. "The only thing that amazes me is that you haven't had worse," he told Father when they ran into each other in the vet-supplies aisle at Burgess Feeds. "You can't interfere with something as God-given as a milking schedule, Reinhard. Not and expect life to go on as normal."

John Hildebrand, our church janitor, was fascinated. "Your cows are practising passive resistance, Brother Niebuhr," he observed. "Elder Ewert taught a Bible study about that just last Thursday. The Mennonites always resisted when governments tried to make them change their faith." He picked up a stack of hymnals and began distributing them into the book-slots of the choir's pews. "You know what your cows are, Brother Niebuhr? They're conscientious objectors! Who knows—maybe cows have religious principles too!"

"They don't seem to be getting used to it," Father finally admitted that fall when the October dairy cheque arrived. "We're losing ground every month."

"Well hey, why don't we just sell the island," I suggested, as if the idea had only just occurred to me.

Father didn't say anything. We all knew he was still working on the stabilizers for the *John 3:16*. And I'd seen drawings—with distances, dimensions—in which the island's size had been more than doubled using cantilevered platforms that extended thirty feet over the ocean on all sides. It was pretty clear what occupied

Father's mind while he washed all those pots and pans at the Harrison Hotel.

"We simply have to find some other way," sighed Mother. "Another few months and we'll be bankrupt for sure."

We all stared at the floor, pretending the only other solution wasn't staring us in the face.

"I have an idea!" said little Heidi who was always best at this sort of thing. "Why don't we milk the cows in the morning and night?"

We all laughed at the disingenuous "we". There was no way the girls were old enough to milk the cows. It took two people to do it, and Mother's fear of cows was legendary. Actually Mother was afraid of almost everything in the animal kingdom. Mice. Chickens. Pigs. Spiders. Just about every creature on a farm except tame cats.

Like Father, Mother really wasn't a farming person. She was an organist, in the wrong place at the wrong time.

But at noon the next day, Mother showed up in the barn. She was dressed in her berry-picking outfit—an old skirt, an old blouse, and a huge straw hat with the fake strawberries torn off.

"All right," she said resolutely, fearfully. "All right. Show me what to do."

On the following weekend, we reverted to normal milking schedules. Father and I milked mornings, and Mother and I milked evenings.

You'd have thought that our cows, having so energetically resisted Father's heresies for half a year, would have taken our return to the Orthodox Schedule with unrestrained joy.

But they didn't. Not really. Milk production increased slightly, but only slightly.

The problem now was Mother.

Mother's efforts were heroic, but she drove the cows crazy. She approached each one of them as if it were a lit stick of dynamite. She scurried for safety at every kick or flick of tail—something her tentative fumblings at their rear ends virtually guaranteed. She kept mixing up the vacuum and pressure hoses on our antiquated vacuum milking system, which blew the teat-cups off their udders and the lids off their milking machines. Our sessions regularly took two hours instead of one, and we invariably left the barn drenched in milk.

Father tried every solution he could think of. He made up several pairs of manacles, connected by a short length of chain, which we slipped over the hind legs of the cows on Mother's side of the barn. (This shortened the reach of their kicks but failed to address the fact that simply their impulse to kick was enough to frighten Mother.) He painted the pressure hoses white and the vacuum hoses red. (We eventually had to conclude that fear made Mother temporarily color-blind.) Father even mocked up a cow's udder with rag-wrapped spindles from an old baby crib, so she could practice applying the teat-cups without a skittish cow at the receiving end. But Mother simply couldn't rid herself of the visceral feeling that so much pull and suction must really hurt a cow's teats. "I mean, wouldn't it yours?" she demanded, folding her arms protectively over her chest.

I stabled the cows in alternate stanchions to keep them farther apart—Mother was particularly afraid of being crushed between them. Father cut holes into the walls of the pig pen so the pigs could be fed without entering the pen. Our rooster—who really did have man-killer instincts—was sentenced to solitary confinement, and the barn-cats were banned from the lower barn.

We were just beginning to make progress—slow, painful progress—when the whole exercise was abruptly rendered academic.

Father lost his job at the Harrison Hotel.

thirteen

It was astonishing how quickly everything unravelled after that.

Mr. James Elliott Tunbridge seemed to know about the hotel lay-offs almost as soon as we did.

Once again he welcomed Father with civility, condolences and gravity. He was, after all, an Elder of the Bank of Montreal. But this time he didn't feel so optimistic.

The numbers, unfortunately, had stopped adding up.

We owed $15,565 on a farm that was worth, with livestock, less than $12,000.

Our remaining equity in Father's island, which Mr. Tunbridge said might be worth another $2,500, didn't cover the difference anymore.

But the biggest problem was our monthly debits: $205.75 against earnings of $137.75—with no realistic hope of improvement.

Under those circumstances, Mr. Tunbridge explained, the bank had no choice but to call in Father's loan.

It did. Repayable in thirty days.

For the next two weeks, it seemed to me that all the nails and screws that held our lives together kept falling out. Pictures fell off the walls. Doors kept falling out of their hinges. That's the way it seemed to me.

Every time I came home from school, new decisions had been made, or were being considered. The farm was being sold. The farm was not being sold. The farm was being traded. No, the farm was being sold, but we were going to rent it back. And so on.

It was as if an invisible shield under which we'd lived—one I'd never been aware of before—had suddenly evaporated. Strangers began to wander through our house whenever they felt like it. They looked into our cupboards. They climbed into our attic. One of them, a man with a thick moustache, looked under my bed.

It really bothered me that he'd looked under my bed.

Little Heidi became confused. "Can I still live in my playhouse?" she asked.

"Yes," I assured her. "No," Gutrun said sadly. We said it at the same time.

Heidi looked from Gutrun to me and then back at Gutrun. There seemed to be some room to maneuver. "Nobody's taking my playhouse," she said fiercely, banging her hand flat on the table just like Father. "Finished!"

Father called Lafreniere to explain that we couldn't manage the car payments anymore. Lafreniere agreed to take back the car and call it even. He said his boys would pick it up on Saturday afternoon.

On Saturday morning, Father was unusually quiet during milking. He had that hangdog look again that I hadn't seen for years. After breakfast he parked the car in front of the house and began to clean it up.

He washed it twice, then waxed both its exterior and its dashboard. He cleaned the windows with vinegar and polished the chrome and the mouldings. He used an old toothbrush to clean right into the corners, and even sanded off some of the rust. He crawled under the chassis to scrub dirt from its muffler and axles.

He didn't ask for help, and I somehow understood he didn't want any.

Then he sat down on the front steps and brooded.

It wasn't the loss of the car that bothered him. I was old enough to understand that now. It was the reneging on the debt. To a Mennonite, the mere taking on of debt was a venture onto morally thin ice, but reneging on a debt brought unequivocal shame. It didn't matter that Lafreniere wasn't losing a nickel on the deal. What mattered was that a promise had been made, and now it had been broken. The humiliation pressed down on Father like a ton of hay.

After a while I crept down the stairs and sat down next to him without saying anything.

He just sat there wordlessly, his hands hanging slack, smelling of wax and vinegar and chrome polish.

We shredded twigs and chewed on grass stalks for a long time.

Finally, he said, "I've always been afraid something like this would happen."

I could only nod in silence. I was too overwhelmed by the way Father was suddenly talking to me like a grownup.

I can't even remember whether he said anything more. It didn't matter, because talking or just sitting, we were doing it together. I wanted desperately to rise to the occasion, but all I could think to say was, "He looked under my bed, Father."

He nodded that he understood. And then we just shredded more twigs until Lafreniere's men showed up. But I came away from that afternoon with a lifetime conviction that there is nothing the world wants more than to breach the sanctity of one's home and inner life, and that, amongst many other ways of dropping one's guard, borrowing money is probably the most effective way of handing over the keys.

When Lafreniere's men arrived—one introduced himself as "Jerry" but I didn't catch the other's name; he wore a brush cut—they were a bit nonplussed at Father's broken-English apologies. "If we haven't got the brucellosis and I am lose the whole herd, everything," he assured them, "not anything like this will happen. I pay every month—every month exact."

He pointed sadly at the car. "She is good car, yes. You just always double-clutch and watch for the brake oil."

The brush cut eyed the old car dubiously. "Whatever you say, mister," he shrugged.

"Sometimes she don't start so good if it makes lots of rain," Father admitted. "But what's to do, you take off the *Zuendverteiler,* the . . . Peter, what's *Zuendverteiler?* yes, distributor, you take off the distributor top, and dry by the stove you see? Just a little by the stove and she goes."

"Will she start now?" the one called Jerry asked.

"Oh *ja*, on a day *mit* only clouds, no trouble," Father assured him. "If they don't laid me off at the hotel, you see, I keep this car long time. I pay every month, always exact. You can ask Mr. Tunbridge at the bank. They sell that hotel to a Danish company you see, and they lay off almost half. I don't be there so very long so I am lay off quick, that's it."

"Well, might as well get a move on," the brush cut said, opening our car's door. "I'll risk it with this one, Jerry; you mop up from behind."

"You always watch the brake oil," Father called after them as they pulled away. "You double-clutch and watch the brake oil; she's very good car!"

Work on the farm, except for the feeding of the animals, stopped completely. Father now spent all his time in town, trying to find work and a buyer for our farm and livestock. He had little luck finding either. There was a recession that year—brief, as it turned out, but Father had no way of knowing that—and livestock prices were low. He finally had to sell our animals in a block to a broker for an upset price.

From his conversations with Mother at night—I often crouched at the top of the stairs—I knew that Father was still hoping to pay off our loan without selling his island. Onkel Jacob didn't see how it could be done, and Mr. Tunbridge said the numbers just weren't there. But one day while hitch-hiking into town, Father was dropped off near the Callaghan Racing Stables on the Lougheed Highway, which gave him an idea he spent several days researching and sketching. Then he had another meeting with our real estate agent.

It took a lot of convincing, but eventually the agent agreed to change our listing from dairy to horse farm. I had a look at Father's drawings on the day the agent came by, and I was amazed. It didn't even look like our farm, but after a while you could see its outlines, or what remained of them, incorporated into a splendid horse farm with a training ring, a horse barn, a tack room and an oval race track. Our slough, which had always been a nuisance during haying or ploughing, now fit into place as though it had been put there by a landscape architect.

"You don't need more than twenty-five acres for a horse farm," Father said. "Those horse people use a different yardstick for such things."

He gave every prospective buyer a set of those sketches.

The result was almost instantaneous. In less than a month, we'd sold our farm to a Vancouver Southlands stable owner for $14,000.

With the proceeds from the sale of our livestock, that brought the amount to $15,840.

Everyone was astounded at this turn of events. "You should have seen that Tunbridge," Onkel Jacob grinned, when he stopped by to help himself to our remaining bales of hay. "I thought his eyes were going to fall out of his head. Two days before the deadline; I think he'd already ordered up the foreclosure papers. Is Reinhard around, Margarete? I thought I'd have a look at some of your milk cans too."

"He's gone to Vancouver," Mother said. "You can have the milk cans, Jacob. Reinhard's gone to Vancouver to look for a job."

Deacon Goertzen, when he dropped by to pick up the vacuum hoses Father had promised him, couldn't suppress his admiration either. "I knew we'd picked the right man for our Fundraising Committee," he grinned. "Selling the idea for a horse farm for $14,000—now that's pure genius. How much do you think I could get for the idea of my farm as an airport?"

When Father telephoned five days later, he and Mother talked for a long time. That evening after supper she gathered us around her the way she'd always done when thunderstorms shook the farm. "Your father hasn't found a job yet, but he's found us a house," she told us, looking almost guilty with relief. "It's in Vancouver. It's not a very nice house, it'll need a lot of fixing up, but at least it'll be a roof over our heads."

"You mean we're not going to be farmers anymore?" Heidi asked fearfully.

"You can't farm in Vancouver, you dummy," Gutrun snorted. "They've got sidewalks."

"Gutrun," Mother warned. "No, sweetheart, we're not going to be farmers anymore."

"Then how will we get to heaven?" Heidi wailed. "And see Oma, and Willy?"

"Reverend Friesen doesn't farm anymore," I pointed out. "And he's for sure going to heaven."

"And anyway, Willy's a dog," Gutrun said.

"Not anymore," Heidi insisted. "He's a angel!"

"Reverend Friesen's going to heaven because he still has a big garden," I explained. "You can still get to heaven if you have a garden. I'll bet we'll have a garden in Vancouver, won't we, Mother?"

The grateful look Mother gave me made me feel about eighteen years old.

"Of course we'll have a garden, *Liebchen*. With lots of peas and carrots, and raspberries and dahlias and sunflowers." She made a quick swipe at a tear that had begun to slide down her cheek. "We'll have a great big garden, with lots of sunshine and good dreams and happiness and music, and a good job for Father—and we'll all get to heaven just like Oma."

"With peas and raspberries and slugs?" Heidi demanded happily. "Oh goody! I love drowning slugs!"

fourteen

For the first four months after we moved to Vancouver, Father had no luck finding a job.

He walked Vancouver's streets from morning till night, searching. Now and then he got a few hours hauling freight or cleaning out basements. He delivered fliers and cut grass. He refused to apply for social assistance.

At home, the pantry emptied and the menu dwindled. Mother kept finding new ways to prepare rice and beans. When we ran out of sawdust for the furnace, Father installed a cast-off tin airtight in the kitchen. We fired it with boards from a collapsed shed on a nearby empty lot.

Seeing how badly Father felt about it all, and how torn between his duties and his dreams, we kept our grumbling to ourselves.

✵

Then on Mother's birthday, May 14, Gutrun, Heidi, Mother and I returned from a Saturday afternoon concert at church to find our windows ablaze with lights, the table set with our Sunday dishes, and the whole house filled with the delicious smell of *Kalbskotlett* and *Schmorkohl.*

"*Um Himmel's Willen!*" Mother gasped, while we kids just gawked. "Reinhard, have you lost your senses?"

"Everybody have a seat," Father instructed, grinning like a barn cat caught in the milkhouse. "The first course will be served in exactly three minutes."

"Jee-whiz!" Heidi crowed, trying out her latest English expression. "Jee-willikers! Where'd you get all this stuff?"

"You sit over here, Mother," Father instructed. "And you there, Peter. Gutrun? Here, please. That's right, Heidi."

"When are we going to be enlightened as to what this is all about?" Mother asked a little anxiously.

"All in good time," Father said. "We'll start with grace. Dear Lord, we thank Thee for Thy love and mercy; we're grateful for the way Thou hast always guided and protected us through trouble and strife. Whenever we were destitute, Thou hast provided a roof over our heads, and when we were hungry, Thou gavest us the means to find food. We thank Thee now for this food before us, which Thou hast provided but which I was too willful to see, and we ask that Thou bless it for the benefit of our bodies. In Jesus's name. Amen."

When we all looked up again, Mother's face had become very sad, and Gutrun's very thoughtful. But Heidi's eyes flashed and she banged her hands on the table. "Let's eat!" she demanded happily. "Did you cook this, Father? Jee willikers, it sure smells good!"

"It's roasted island with ocean sauce," Father said with a grin that wobbled just a touch around the edges. "You're going to love it."

"You bet!" Heidi enthused. "Give me lots!"

"You always say 'please', Heidi," Mother admonished automatically, but more quietly than usual.

Gutrun had become very serious and her voice was solemn. "You've sold your island, haven't you Father?" she asked.

"Our island," Father agreed. "And you won't believe how much we got for it."

"You mean we're eating Father's island?" Heidi demanded, her eyes suddenly large.

"That's right," Father said more firmly, taking up a pot and handing it to Mother. "This is the grassy part on the top, the part with the bushes that look like boysenberry, and these," he pointed at the big dish of *Kotletts*, "are some of the rocks from its south side. Now we're going to keep having island for dinner until I find a job, because I've thought about it and I've prayed about it, and I'm convinced the Lord doesn't want us to starve while we're waiting. Now, who wants some rocks?"

Three weeks later, Father landed a job at a sash & door company, making wooden ladders.

✵

Years later, long after Father's death, I was ocean fishing with some English friends off Baline Bay when I got my third and final look at Father's island. It was about ten miles off our starboard bow, visible primarily because it now had a large house on it, and as we cruised closer, I grinned to see that its intricate construction included lots of cantilevered decks and platforms, virtually doubling the island's size. There was also a floating dock with a beautifully restored 1937 Chriscraft Redoubtable tied up to it, and it was that boat that convinced me, on impulse, to put our dinghy over the side and motor over for a visit.

The owners, Edward and Jennifer Windsor, were pleased to fill me in on what they knew of the island's history. They had bought it as raw land some eight years earlier from a businessman named Taylor for $1.3 million, and had hired a marine architect to design their home and dock. It had taken three years to build and there had been plenty of technical problems, not the least of which involved the island's unstable eastern shoreline. They'd had to haul in fifteen barge-loads of rocks to deal with that.

The little island now had a name, which they'd chosen from a sign they'd found pounded into its highest point—an old, much-weathered sign that had appealed as much to their sense of sentiment as their sense of history. It had seemed to them, in some ineffable way, to summarize some early pioneer's dreams for the place, and so they'd rescued and framed it for posterity. They took me down to their den and showed it to me, hanging over a large stone fireplace.

I already knew the sign of course.

A four-feet-by-four-foot square of plywood with Onkel Jacob's now barely legible admonition scrawled in my spelling and handwriting across the top: *No Trespissing.* But below that I was startled to find, in much bolder, clearer black stove paint—paint that appeared to have been renewed on one or even several occasions—the words: ST. CHRISTOPH'S EILAND.

And that lettering was unmistakably Father's.

RENOVATING HEAVEN

one

My father's relationship with the Rest of the World was never very comfortable.

This was, for the most part, quite intentional. Mennonites had always been told to avoid excessive contact with "The World", and Father took that instruction quite seriously. Mennonites had also always been highly suspicious of both secular and religious governments—especially the latter. "No middlemen between the believer and his God" was their rallying cry—causing my Onkel Jacob to exclaim, "Will you look at that! Already back in the sixteenth century we were trying to buy everything wholesale—even our religion!"

After almost a decade in Canada, during which we'd lived on three different farms in British Columbia, Father still spoke virtually no English, knew no "Englishers," and still used Onkel Jacob for all his dealings with government bureaucracies.

Maintaining that level of isolation in farming country had been easy, but now, in South Vancouver, where everyone lived cheek by jowl and the jobs were mostly in manufacturing, Father found contact with The World almost unavoidable. And there was another difference he hadn't anticipated. On a farm, everyone's energies were mostly focussed on the farm's operations rather than the condition of its buildings. In a city, your house was all you had. In the absence of any other common language, it was your house that told your neighbours everything about you.

I think our entire family grasped this concept intuitively, but as a fourteen-year-old boy my grasp was more straightforward than Father's. For me, our new house was simply an embarrassment. For weeks I pleaded and cajoled, offering to strip its peeling asbestos tiles or paint its disintegrating window frames. I said I'd get an after school job and pay for the paint myself. I offered to dig up the weed-infested front yard and plant a proper lawn. I thought we could replace its trampled chicken wire fence with mill ends from a sawmill at the foot of Fraser Street.

Father showed some brief interest in the notion of a proper lawn, but even that, he explained, would have to wait. He had a plan, an integrated design, a Vision for the whole place—so there was no point in doing anything piecemeal. Things had to be done in the proper sequence.

Impatience just wasted money. There was no point in stripping the tiles when they'd only be torn off and replaced with stucco anyway. That wouldn't happen right away, of course; the interior would come first, the uneven floors, the rusted-out plumbing. There would be plenty for me to do just helping him replace the plaster & lath walls. If I had extra time on my hands, there'd be plenty of studs to de-nail and the nails to straighten.

Getting ahead of ourselves would only cause more problems down the road.

I rolled my eyes and appealed to Mother. She must have known there was no way I'd ever make any friends living in a shack like ours. But Mother just shook her head. I couldn't really tell whose side she was on, but she knew better than to challenge Father once he had a plan. We all did.

And anyway, it wasn't the plan that was the problem. Father's plans usually made sense. This one certainly did. We all wanted a nice house. The problem was that Father's plans always took forever. They took a hundred million years.

"If that man had to build a box for no other reason than to carry a load of shit from the barn to the manure pile and then throw it away," I once overheard my Onkel Jacob grumble to Mother, "he'd still take a decade and build it to rival the Ark of the Covenant. That man's incapable of building for less than eternity, Margarete." Onkel Jacob had been waiting for his promised bathroom cabinet for over a year. "He's got the cart before the horse. Eternity comes after life on earth—and I was planning to live them in that order!"

It wasn't even that I didn't understand Father's point of view. Mother had already explained it to me several times. After searching for almost half a year for a job in Vancouver, Father had finally found one at the MacDonald Sash & Door Company. The MacDonald Sash

& Door Company didn't actually make doors, it made wooden ladders, but the point was, Father was finally going to be working with wood again. His training in cabinet-building back in Germany was finally going to be utilized. Deep down he'd always hated farming, and would never have agreed to do it if it hadn't been the only basis on which the Canadian government had let us immigrate.

But making ladders the Canadian way had turned out to be a huge disappointment. "The way they slap those things together, they're worse than junk," he'd reported to Mother after his first day at work. "Rotten wood, splintery dowels, no bolts, everything just stiffened with cheap glue. Store a ladder like that in a damp shed for a month and it'd fall apart the first time you stepped on it!"

Even at my age I knew what that meant. In our house, sloppiness was next to Godlessness. Father talked about sloppiness the way Elder Friesen talked about mortal sin.

So our house, Mother had explained to me, was going to be Father's answer to the MacDonald Sash & Door Company. Or actually, his answer to the Rest of the World. Every line would be plumb. Every angle would be precise. A marble dropped on the floor wouldn't know which way to roll. It would be Father's "triumph and absolution" she explained. I nodded sadly. I didn't really understand what she meant by triumph and absolution but I had a pretty good idea how long they would take to achieve. And with his job, Father would only be able to renovate evenings and weekends.

I contemplated rebellion and insurrection. I fantasized buying five-gallon pails of paint and slathering the entire exterior on a weekend when Father wasn't home. I imagined organizing a work party of my friends, transfiguring the front yard in a gardening blitzkrieg. I knew it would all be temporary—wasteful and sinful, a fake facade over imprecision and corruption—but I didn't care. I was prepared to answer for that. Anything was better than having to live the rest of my life in this humiliating hovel.

But my fantasies never progressed past the imagining stage. I hadn't yet made any friends in this city, and anyway, Father never went away for weekends.

two

Mother had promised my sisters Gutrun and Heidi that when we moved to the city, we'd still have a big garden. With a big garden, she'd assured them, we'd still qualify as farmers and could still get to heaven.

But this garden also fell victim to Father's master plan. There'd be a garden eventually, of course, but it would have to wait until the garage was torn down, and for the moment there were more important things on Father's list than tearing down the garage. So Mother suggested we keep a couple of rabbits instead.

Father was dubious, but Gutrun was delighted and little Heidi was ecstatic. I was delegated to build the rabbit hutch, so I was also pleased. It gave me a legitimate reason to use Father's tools—something he rarely permitted. It also gave me a legitimate reason to tear down the front yard fence—I'd need that chicken wire for the rabbit run. I was pretty sure Father wouldn't spring for new chicken wire.

I was right on all counts. Clearly, Father was really preoccupied. He barely looked up from his drawings and measurements when I made off with his sledgehammer and crowbar. He didn't supervise my attack on the back wall of the garage for a supply of boards for the hutch. He virtually ignored me as I rummaged around in his nail supply for shingle nails.

I finished the hutch in about a week. It looked great to me. I'd taken considerable pains with the measuring and cutting, and had even used a right-angle to make everything square. The rabbit run took only two additional days. It was a narrow wire corridor about ten feet long, framed with old studs and separated from the hutch by a guillotine door. Heidi could barely contain herself.

"Is that where they'll go for their picnics?" she demanded, her little body bobbing and squirming with excitement. "Is that where they'll have their races?"

Even Father seemed impressed. He only pointed out four things I'd gotten wrong. He asked me where I'd left his fencing pliers and his level. He said there wasn't much point in owning tools if you could never find them. Fortunately Gutrun found them right inside the hutch where they hadn't gotten wet. That was the only place I hadn't looked.

If I'd had any idea how much trouble they would get me into over the next couple of months, I'd never have offered to find us the rabbits. For one thing, I hadn't realized how hard it would be to find pet rabbits in a city. In farming country it would have been a simple matter of asking around at school. A lot of farmers kept rabbits, and somebody was always giving some away. But at our school in Vancouver I couldn't find anyone who knew of any rabbits. I asked around at church too, with no better luck.

Then somebody suggested Laundromats.

I'd never heard of Laundromats, but once I'd found several on Fraser Street, I began to monitor their bulletin boards. And sure enough, three weeks later I saw an announcement: *THREE CHINCHILLA GRAY TICKED RABBITS, ONE MALE, TWO FEMALE, FREE TO GOOD HOME, 499 East 55th Avenue.* The address was only about six blocks from our place.

"Oh yeah, these'll give you plenty of excitement," the man who answered the door chuckled, pulling one out of its cage. He looked like Deacon Doerksen with his bald head and lumpy nose. The rabbit looked awfully big. "Regular little Houdinis, these rascals. Did you bring a box?"

I hadn't. Actually, I'd only meant to have a look and then report back. But everything just seemed to happen without stopping. Ten minutes later I was walking up Prince Edward Street carrying a box full of three struggling rabbits.

"Guess what I've got," I said to Heidi when I got home. The rabbits in the box thumped and scratched. Heidi's eyes became huge. "We've got rabbits, we've got rabbits," she shrieked, trying to thrust her fingers into the box. Mother came in from the kitchen; Father came up from the basement. I opened the box carefully, keeping the flaps upright so the rabbits wouldn't jump out.

"The notice in the Laundromat said they were Chinchillas, but the man called them Houdinis," I said.

Father actually laughed. Mother smiled.

"What?" I demanded.

Father said Houdini had been a famous escape artist in the '20s. Even Mennonites knew about him. He said I'd better make sure my hutch was really escape-proof. Heidi looked worried.

"They'll never get out of that hutch," I assured her. "How could they possibly get through all that wood and wire?"

The next morning the hutch was empty and the rabbits were gone.

Father pointed to a hole they'd burrowed under the frame of the run. He said I'd probably have to set the run on a brick or stone foundation.

I found the rabbits munching grass in the ditch that ran along our back alley. I caught the first two fairly easily, but it took me over an hour to get the third one safely back into the hutch. I didn't let them out into their run until I'd built a brick foundation under its frame.

The next day they were gone again. This time they'd found and stretched a small gap in the chicken wire.

I closed the gap and recaptured them. They got out again two days later by chewing through a wooden slat. A week later they knocked out a knot in a board and enlarged the hole.

I can't remember how they got out the next time, or the next, or the next. No matter how much I fixed and reinforced their cage, they kept finding ways to get out.

"They're regular escape artists all right," Mother smiled. Heidi laughed. "That one there's Hootie," she said. "And that one's Tootie. He's the worstest one." Gutrun grinned. Everybody seemed to find this escaping business funny except me. I was the one who always had to chase after them.

Eventually I did start gaining on our Houdinis. Their escapes dropped from every few days to every few weeks. I buried the chicken wire more than a foot deep all around their run and even covered the hutch with it. I found some more old bricks and paved the entire bottom of their run. I attached a spring to their hutch door and put a lock on it.

That August our next-door neighbour at number 430, Mr. Henry Windebank, stopped by to talk to Father. He wanted to discuss the fence between our houses. It was in sorry shape and needed replacing. He reminded Father that every property owner was responsible for the fence on his west side. He said he was planning to have his yard landscaped and his old lawn replaced, and he hoped Father would consider replacing the fence at the same time.

I don't think Father knew about being responsible for our west side fence and I suspected it wasn't very high on his renovation list, but I could see that he didn't want to have a fight with Mr. Windebank. So we spent the following Saturday digging out crumbling fence posts and smashing apart the sections in between. For the rest of the week, from after school until it got dark, I got to burn the piles of rotten boards we'd heaped up along the property line, which I enjoyed. I even got the job done by the next weekend like I'd promised, although on one of the days Mrs. Windebank got upset about the smoke dirtying the washing on her clothesline, which I hadn't noticed.

And then the summer ended a lot faster than anyone expected, which meant Mr. Windebank's new lawn didn't really get a chance to green up before the fall rains started, and pretty soon everything was sopping wet and muddy. The runoff cut crooked little creeks all over our backyard, and after a while I had to jump from rock to rock to take our garbage to the garbage can in the alley.

I was in the middle of doing my English homework in the dining room when Heidi burst in, not even taking off her boots or raincoat. "It's Hootie," she gasped, waving a broken stick that sprayed water all over my books. "She's gotten out, and that dog from across the street is chasing her!"

I didn't stop to ask questions. The terrier from the family that had recently moved into number 431 had immediately become the scourge of the neighbourhood, knocking over garbage cans, scattering their contents, and chasing everybody's cats and dogs. As I raced outside I caught sight of him just disappearing around the back of our house. I gave chase, but only managed to catch up because both Hootie and the dog had reversed direction somewhere in the backyard and were now high-tailing it back.

By this time Hootie had given up trying to hide and was just trying to outrace the dog. At the sight of me standing directly in her path she shot almost two feet into the air, made the most amazing mid-air turn, and was churning away at a perfect right angle, her back feet throwing up a spray of mud and pebbles almost before she hit the ground. The terrier tried changing direction just as fast but he lost traction and skidded wide. I charged after Hootie, trying my best to keep her madly bobbing tail in view. The terrier was coming up fast from behind.

I don't remember when the thought struck me that something was terribly wrong. I'd been so intent on the chase that I'd paid no attention to where it was going. I ran three or four more steps and then stopped. Hootie disappeared. The terrier rushed past me and disappeared. I was left standing in the middle of Mr. Windebank's freshly sown lawn, up to my knees in churned-up mud.

Behind me a brutally stark line of deeply punched footsteps led back across the lawn, over the property line and into my own back yard. The evidence couldn't have been more incriminating.

I made a few half-hearted tries at filling in the nearest hole, but that just made things worse.

I tried to turn around by stepping into the already existing holes, but the pattern was maddeningly reversed. Now my right foot was on the wrong side of my body, and my left foot wouldn't fit into my right footprint.

It was hopeless.

I looked over at Mr. Windebank's house but his curtains were motionless. I looked over toward my house, expecting to see the same. What I saw instead was Father, standing large as life in the middle of our living room window. The expression on his face was terrifying.

As I made another move to retrace my steps he yanked open the window. "Stop!" he ordered, aiming a devastating finger down at me. "Don't move! I'm coming down."

I stood there paralyzed, listening to his thundering footsteps on the stairs.

But when he arrived and looked the situation over, there wasn't much he could do. No matter what I tried, the mess just got bigger. By the time I'd made it back to our yard, it looked as if I'd dragged a stone-boat or a cow carcass across the Windebank lawn.

Father just shook his head. "Get yourself cleaned up," was all he said.

By the time I'd cleaned my boots and returned upstairs, Father had sized up the situation, and it looked grim. Windebank would sue us within an inch of our lives. We wouldn't be able to pay, and we'd probably lose the house. Or we'd be in debt to lawyers forever after. Once those wolves got their fangs into you, Father said, they never let go, everyone knew that. Falling into the hands of officials or bureaucrats was more dangerous than falling into the clutches of the Antichrist. Why on earth had he ever agreed to let us have those *verflixte* rabbits in the first place?

I offered, timidly, to go apologize to Mr. Windebank.

"Apologize?" Father snorted. "Of course you should apologize. But that's not going to make any difference.

Apologies don't make the slightest difference once lawyers are involved."

And the more Father thought about it, the worse the scenario became. Once we'd been sued in court, he realized, we'd have a record, and once we had a record, our hope for Canadian citizenship was out the window. How likely was it that Canada would grant citizenship to people with a criminal record? Not a chance, that's what. All our hopes and dreams for a new start in a civilized country—even if it was full of Englishers—right out the window. And why? All because he'd foolishly agreed to let us have a bunch of *verfluchte* rabbits.

"I'll go apologize to Mr. Windebank right now," I said, pulling on my raincoat. "Maybe then he won't sue us and take away our house."

I rang Mr. Windebank's doorbell about a hundred times, but there was nobody home.

By the time I got back to our house, Father's take on our situation had reached catastrophic levels. It wasn't just a matter of not getting our citizenship. It was a lot worse than that. He had just realized that once we had a criminal record, we would be subject to deportation. That's what they did with immigrants who fell afoul of the law. He remembered an emigration officer warning us about that back in Hamburg. We'd be sent back on the *Beaverbrae*, straight back to Germany, which wouldn't want us, had never wanted us because we were pacifists who wouldn't serve in the army, and now, with a criminal record, would definitely not want to have anything to do with us. And then where would we go? We'd probably spend the rest of our lives as Displaced Persons in some hopeless refugee camp in Prussia or Poland.

And all because he hadn't had the foresight to get rid of those *verdammte* English rabbits!

"I'll go out and see if Mr. Windebank's back home yet," I said, hurriedly putting my raincoat back on. "Maybe he's gotten back home already."

He hadn't, but I didn't have the courage to go home and listen to Father anymore. I just stood out on our porch and watched the Windebanks' house for about three hours. I thought I'd see them walking up their sidewalk and then I'd apologize, but finally their front light came on so I guess they must have driven in from the back. I rushed over to their front door and pushed the doorbell, but when the door opened and Mr. Windebank was standing there, I got so confused, I talked to him in German. "*Den Rasen,*" I said, pointing desperately into the dark. "*Ich habe euren Rasen kaputt gemacht. Es tut mir schrecklich leid.*"

"What's he saying?" Mrs. Windebank asked, coming up behind her husband. I kept pointing. "Why is that boy crying, Henry?"

Mr. Windebank had already looked in the direction I was pointing. "Did your rabbits get out again, Peter?" he asked, shading his eyes against the porch light. He didn't sound terribly angry. "Well, we'll have to do a little patching after the grass comes up, that's clear, but there's not much point doing anything until spring. Too wet right now. Too muddy." He clapped me good-humoredly on the shoulder. "Nothing to get all upset about, my lad. Not the end of the world." He turned me around and aimed me back toward our house. "You be sure to tell your parents hello from me now, you hear?"

For a moment I just stood there stunned, staring wildly up into his eyes. Then I bounded home like a chased rabbit. As I yanked off my raincoat I could hear Father talking in the kitchen to Mother. He was telling her to phone Pastor Driediger at the Mennonite Brethren Church. He said the Mennonite Brethren were far more likely to have lawyers in their congregation than our Mennonite Conference. He wanted her to write to Onkel Jacob too, because Onkel Jacob understood the deviousness of Canadian criminal law, and he was on a first-name basis with John Diefenbaker.

"It's okay, Father!" I shouted from the doorway. "It's alright! Mr. Windebank isn't going to sue!"

"Don't interrupt, Peter," Father said tiredly. "You've caused enough trouble for one day already. Margarete, if you think the mail might be too slow, we might have to telephone Jacob tomorrow."

"But Father! I apologized to Mr. Windebank! I apologized, and Mr. Windebank said it was okay."

"Did you hear him, Reinhard?" Mother said, sounding anxious.

"Did I hear what?"

"Mr. Windebank isn't going to sue," I said. "I talked to him, and he isn't going to sue."

"Who's not suing?" Father demanded.

"Mr. Windebank."

Father looked exasperated. "And how would you know a thing like that?"

"I just talked to him."

"What? When?"

"A few minutes ago. He said he wasn't going to sue."

There was a long silence, or so it seemed to me, and then Father pulled over a chair and sat down. He sat down like a sack of potatoes, as if all the strength had gone out of him. He didn't say anything; he just sat there staring at Mother's hands in an unfocussed way. And the strange thing was, I couldn't tell whether he was relieved or disappointed.

Finally he turned to me. "He said that, did he?"

"Yes, Father."

"You're sure you didn't misunderstand?"

"No, Father."

"Because those Englishers, when they start talking fast, you can never be sure exactly what they're saying."

I tried hard to remember what Mr. Windebank had said.

"He said it wasn't time for the end of the world yet."

Father snorted. "I suppose he'd have to hope that's true."

He didn't move for a while longer, and then he shrugged. "Well, at least that gives us some breathing room." He got up slowly, almost painfully. "Because you never know about the English. They'll say something one day, and then the very next . . ."

Mother and I watched his back disappearing down the basement stairs.

Mother turned to the sink and resumed washing pots.

"So Mr. Windebank said it wasn't time for the world to end?"

Her voice was gentle; I couldn't tell whether she was relieved or amused.

"Maybe not until spring," I had to admit. "He said it wouldn't be the end of the world until spring."

three

After two years of renovating, the "grudge match between Father and the English" (as Onkel Jacob put it) was well under way. The floors in the living room and dining room had been pulled up, the joists shimmed level and the floors put down again. The plaster & lath dividing wall between those two rooms had been replaced by a drywall arch, and the kitchen gutted and its counters and cabinets replaced. Both bedrooms, however, were still untouched. So was the bathroom.

So was the entire exterior of the house, except that now it looked even worse.

And then there was the closed-in verandah at the back of the house, a ramshackle structure Father intended to tear off and replace with a full basement-to-attic house extension. This would produce a breakfast nook and third bedroom above, and a high-ceilinged workshop below. The idea was to have a bedroom for the girls, one for my parents and one for me. For the time being, I slept on an army cot in a curtained-off section of the verandah.

At first, we'd all accepted Father's dictum that renovating the house constituted our family's highest priority. This meant that as soon as Father came home from work, we were all on standby, ready to help with whatever work was on his agenda. But it soon became obvious that there was precious little that Gutrun and Heidi could realistically contribute, and Mother had a long list of other urgent responsibilities on her plate.

This left me as Father's main helper—but since Father rarely trusted me to tackle anything on my own, I found myself spending most of my time idly watching as he worked himself to the bone. After a while I convinced him to let me set up a card table nearby so I could do my homework and still be on call if he needed anything held or fetched.

That, in retrospect, proved to be the beginning of my writing career. Reading novels from the Fraser Street Library (especially when cloaked in school textbook covers) and scribbling poems into old school notebooks looked indistinguishable from real homework to Father.

Like most Mennonites of his generation, Father had the gravest doubts about writers. For Mennonites, "writer" was virtually synonymous with "liar" and "rascal". Writers made things up—they lied—and they seemed to have an irresistible inclination toward the disreputable. This was admittedly hearsay—we'd never knowingly harboured a writer in our family tree—but it was better to be safe than sorry. If Father had had any inkling that such subversion was being practised right under his nose, he might have taken a very different approach to my education.

If he'd ever met me on the street after school, he'd have been quickly tipped off, but such was the glorious anonymity of city life that he never did, and I was able to take full advantage of its cover. I had by this time found an after-school job with a firm that imported German records, stereos and television sets, and while I was supposed to contribute all my earnings to the family coffers, I was paid in cash, which allowed for a certain amount of slippage.

As a result I headed off for school every morning to all appearances a decently dressed, obedient Mennonite boy, but emerged from my friend Fred Myers' basement bedroom half an hour later wearing a metallic rayon shirt with raised collar, tight black jeans, Cuban-heeled boots and a heavily Brylcreemed ducktail. It didn't manage to make me any more popular than I already wasn't, but it convinced me that I was undeniably on the move. As the novelist Bert Wilkinson once said, the urge to write can express itself in the strangest currencies.

By now, Father and I were often at loggerheads. I seemed to be developing every characteristic that was likely to offend him. He considered me sloppy, imprecise, hasty, shallow, insincere, disobedient, disrespectful and lazy. He found my susceptibility to the blandishments of English culture alarming, and my interest in the arts an obvious ploy to avoid real work.

It didn't help that he was probably right on most counts.

At one point, after I'd expressed an interest in photography, Mother took me aside and reminded me that Father had been an avid photographer in his youth. In fact, he still had the makings of a darkroom packed up in boxes in the basement. She thought I might consider using this common interest to improve our relationship.

I joined the Photography Club at school and told Father about it. He looked dubious, but thoughtful. I described some of the darkroom techniques they were using, and his eyes seemed to light up. I asked him if I could buy myself an inexpensive camera with some of my earnings and maybe we could set up his darkroom in the basement.

His face fell. He pointed out that, once again, I was putting the cart before the horse. Before buying a camera and impulsively exposing film, I needed to become a lot more familiar with photographic theory. First learn the science, then apply it, he said. He suggested I find a book on photography in the library and study that.

The next day after school Mother said she had a surprise for me. She gave it to me as if it was a box of chocolates. It was a fat German textbook on photography that Father had found in one of his darkroom boxes. Her face was bright with enthusiasm and hope.

I struggled with the book for several days. I found it virtually incomprehensible. While I was quite capable of reading German novels and even poetry, scientific German was beyond me. But even written in English

I would have found it impenetrable. It was obviously written for professional photographers.

"I can't make it through this book, Father," I finally told him. "It's far too complicated. I'll try to find a simpler book in the library."

Mother told me sadly the next day that Father thought my interest in photography "wasn't serious".

That also proved to be an accurate prophecy.

four

By the time Father had finished wiring and dry-walling the two bedrooms at the front of our house, we had been living in Vancouver for over three years.

At this point even my card table had disappeared, so most evenings Father worked alone. When the rest of us returned from our various evening activities, we invariably dropped in to check on his progress and admire his handiwork—but for the most part, Father's renovations had become largely a kind of background noise.

That's why, on returning home one evening after attending a symphony concert, we were startled to discover Father sitting idly in the dark of the living room, listening to the radio.

It was a broadcast of live music, a brass concert of some sort. Probably Johann Strauss.

We all exclaimed at the novelty of seeing Father being idle.

Father looked embarrassed, or maybe guilty. "I just like that kind of music," he shrugged. "I turned on the radio to check an electrical circuit, and then I . . . left it on."

"And sat on the sofa listening," Gutrun agreed. "That's amazing, Father."

"It's not as if I waste time every day," Father pointed out, looking uncomfortable.

We all chorused that nobody was complaining, that we thought it was wonderful that he allowed himself to take a little time off now and then.

The next day, after school, Mother called us kids together for a family discussion. She wanted to propose the idea that we—somehow—buy Father a stereo set.

"He never buys anything for himself," she pointed out. "I had no idea he likes brass music."

"That's because he never wants anything," Heidi agreed.

"A stereo set would cost an awful lot of money," Gutrun worried.

I said that I'd seen them at the Fraser Book & Record Company, where I worked, for about six hundred dollars.

"He'd never spend that kind of money on a stereo," Gutrun warned.

Everyone knew that was true.

"Well, we'll just have to pray about it and keep our eyes open," Mother decided. "Somehow we have to make it happen."

✲

I didn't pray about it, but I did spend some time thinking it over. You could get a stereo set for a lot less than six hundred dollars, but I suspected Father wouldn't be able to get over the shoddy cabinetry. A really good second-hand set wouldn't cost six hundred dollars either, but I suspected it would still cost more than Father would be willing to spend. What we really needed was an inexplicable gift from God for ninety-nine dollars and ninety-nine cents, tax included.

"Don't mock, Peter," Mother said when I passed on my thoughts. "Something will come up; you'll see."

And of course it did, though I no longer recall exactly who came up with the idea. It may have been my Onkel Heinrich, who worked for an electronics firm in Victoria and whom we consulted at various stages in the process. In any case, somebody suggested HEATHKIT, a company that produced high-quality amplifier kits that you assembled yourself, following numbered directions in an instruction booklet. Onkel Heinrich assured us that it was absolutely idiot-proof, and the price was only $59.95.

"After that you'll still need a record player and some speakers, and I don't know what you'll want to do about the cabinetry," Onkel Heinrich said. "From what I know of Reinhard, wouldn't he want to build the cabinet himself?"

When we finally broached the subject with Father, that's what eventually clinched the deal. At first, as expected, he wouldn't hear of it, but when he realized he could save more than half the purchase price by building much of it himself, and when a cousin in Winnipeg offered to get him the player and speakers wholesale, bringing the entire cost to a mere $275.00, Father finally let us talk him into it.

The speakers were the first to arrive: big fifteen-inch Wharfdales that looked imposing just sitting there in their cardboard boxes. The amplifier came next, a frightening array of electronic components and circuit boards packed into a reassuringly uncomplicated-looking outer case. Finally, a Dual automatic turntable—futuristic, racy and expensive-looking. I examined them all several times when no one else was home.

Father built the two speaker cabinets first, and then a third for the amplifier and turntable. He made them all out of sheets of birch plywood he selected himself, fussily, obsessively, driving the salesman at Fraser Building Supplies crazy. He worked slowly and precisely, making no concessions to time or difficulty. All cabinet walls were joined by mortises and tenons; all drawers were exquisitely dovetailed and glued. The cabinet backs were drilled and secured with a necklace of wood screws, and the bottoms of the speaker cabinets filled and anchored with fifty pounds of fine sand. When all the cabinets were finally done, almost a year later, he finished each one of them with four separately buffed layers of spar varnish.

The assembling of the amplifier wasn't quite as idiot-proof as Onkel Heinrich had insisted, but once we'd dragooned him into helping, it might as well have been.

When everything was ready, Father installed the

speakers, amplifier and turntable into the cabinets as per Onkel Heinrich's instructions. Then, on September 21, Father's birthday, Mother baked a cake, we all ate it, Father prayed his usual twenty-minute special-event prayer, and then we assembled in our livingroom for the big test.

Mother had bought our first record—Haydn's Concerto for Trumpet & Orchestra in E-flat Major—especially for the occasion. Father hoisted it onto the turntable, pressed the PLAY button and set the volume to #6. We all leaned forward expectantly.

The first blast of the trumpet almost blew us out of our seats. Father hastily turned the volume down to #4. The next salvo washed over us with the force of a musical tidal wave. Father hesitated, then turned the volume down to #3. For the rest of the record we just sat there amazed, transfixed by the trumpet's splendid stentorian authority, its glorious clarion call. It soared above the violins like a great effortless bird, circling and swooping, plunging and exalting, until the two, like earth and sky, finally came together in one great harmonious swirling, a torrential musical waterfall that stunned us with its magnificence.

The speakers hissed emptily. For a moment, nobody said anything. Then Heidi burst out, "Ho-lee cheese-whiz willikers! That even sounds better than church!"

"Heidi," Mother remonstrated, though she didn't really look offended. Father was actually smiling, and Gutrun was hugging herself happily. I was trying to figure out when there'd be nobody home so I could borrow an Elvis record and play it at volume #7.

"It does sound fairly good, doesn't it," Father acknowledged.

"It's magnificent, Reinhard," Mother said fervently. "It's absolutely the most magnificent thing I've ever heard."

"Well, I don't know about that," Father said, but it was pretty obvious he was inclined to agree.

We played that record three more times that evening, and over the next several weeks Mother found excuses to invite half the congregation over for *Kaffee und Strudel*, to listen to Father's amazing stereo. One evening our guests even included Mr. Manfred Meier, the owner of the Fraser Book & Record Company, who wasn't Mennonite but he was German, so it was alright. He joked he'd heard so much about Father's stereo set, he simply had to drop in to "check on the competition".

"It's really no big thing," Father demurred, genuinely embarrassed. "We shouldn't be making all this fuss about it."

Mr. Meier disagreed. "This cabinetry is superb," he said, running an expert hand over the finish. "My most expensive line isn't even this good." He became very animated. "Would you consider building me a set—just the cabinet I mean—for my own home?"

Father was flustered but clearly pleased. The two men sat down in a corner to discuss designs. Mother was so excited that even I noticed it.

"Your face is really pink, Mother," I told her, but she just shushed me.

For the next several Sunday nights, when the rest of us came home from our various evening choir and orchestra practises, we found Father sitting quietly in the dark, listening to his stereo. He still looked somewhat guilty about it, but he couldn't have worked on the house on Sunday nights anyway. He was a calmer man on these evenings, gentler, not so gloomy. Mother often joined him on the sofa for another hour or so, before they went to bed. They made such a nice picture, sitting there contentedly listening to the music, that I didn't care as much about how rotten our house still looked on the outside.

I can't remember exactly when it happened—it would have been a couple of months or so later—that I came home from a school play one evening to discover Father with his head deep in the amplifier cabinet. There were bits of amplifier parts strewn all over the living-room floor.

"What's going on?" I demanded.

Father didn't answer. He may not have heard me.

Mother was in the kitchen looking worried. "Onkel Heinrich finally came by to hear how the stereo sounded," she said. "And I don't know, I wasn't there, but Father said that Onkel Heinrich said that there was something wrong with the bass."

"Something wrong with the bass?" I repeated, dumbly, because it made absolutely no sense. "What could possibly be wrong with that bass? It sounds better than the pipe organ at the Ryerson United."

Mother twisted the water out of a dishcloth and shook it vigorously. "That's what I told him too—but I don't think he's listening. He takes Onkel Heinrich's word as gospel on this subject."

That made me so mad, I probably went a little overboard. "Onkel Heinrich is so full of it he squishes," I said loudly to Father's back, in the living room. "What does he know about music anyway? He's just a guy who fixes stupid radios in Victoria!"

Father pulled his head carefully out of the amplifier cabinet and looked around at me—unhappy, irritated. "For a start, you can keep a civil tongue in your head," he said curtly. "Your Onkel Heinrich virtually built this amplifier. He knows what he's talking about."

"No he doesn't," I insisted, startled at my defiance but incapable of controlling it. "He knows about electronics, but he doesn't know anything about music. There's a big difference!"

Father snorted. "And I suppose two years of music lessons makes you an expert."

"No," I insisted. "But I know about this. That bass is just fine. It sounds just great. Mother thinks so too."

Father's face closed. "Heinrich knows his business, and if he says there's something wrong with the bass, it means I've made a mistake in the assembly somewhere. Talking isn't going to make any difference. I'm going to take it apart and get it right. That's all there is to it." He stuck his head back into the cabinet.

I was dismissed.

When Father had reassembled the amplifier, it sounded exactly the same as before.

By now even Onkel Heinrich seemed to have recognized his blunder and tried to tell Father it sounded okay, but Father concluded Onkel Heinrich was just losing his nerve and he didn't believe him. He took apart the amplifier for a third time, carefully identifying each part so that he wouldn't need Onkel Heinrich's help again, and when he'd reassembled everything once more, it did sound different—it sounded worse.

At this point Father gave up. He'd begun to suspect, he told Mother, that God was showing him the folly of giving in to one's vain and idle desires. He'd spent over a year and a half on this project—an appalling waste of time and money. There were more important things to accomplish, and he was going back to accomplishing them.

Two days later he began ripping up the bathroom floor.

Father never played his stereo again, but the rest of us did. Even with its slightly compromised bass it still sounded pretty darn good. Mother and I often played the classical records we bought from the Fraser Book and Record Company, where I got everything at 40% off.

Whenever Father walked past the living room while we were playing the records, he'd stop briefly, listen carefully, shake his head and walk on.

five

I can still remember the day Father announced that he was starting Phase Three of our house renovation. This would involve tearing off the closed-in verandah, and replacing it with a fifteen-foot house extension.

I hadn't even known there'd been a Phase One and Two. Even Mother seemed surprised. But the point was, Father was going to use his upcoming two-week annual holiday to accomplish this enormous task. It would be the first time Father would be laying a hand on our house's exterior "in anger," as Onkel Jacob put it, since we'd bought the place.

I couldn't see how Father could possibly accomplish all this in a mere two weeks, until he told me that he'd hired Frank Epp to help him during that time.

That opened up a whole new set of possibilities.

One was that we'd actually find ourselves, at the end of two weeks, with at least a roughed in, roofed-over addition nailed to the end of our house—which Father would then take his usual hundred million years to finish.

Another was that we might find ourselves under a gigantic tarp in a semi-destroyed house, shivering through the winter.

A third—that we'd be living in some relative's basement because Frank Epp had accidentally burned down our house—could also not be entirely discounted.

Frank Epp was notorious around our church for two essentially incompatible characteristics. He was a tireless and very fast worker, who cut first and thought about it later. Since Father always thought five times before he cut, I couldn't see how Father could possibly work with Frank Epp.

Things became clearer when Father told me he'd recently met Frank at a Bible study class. Frank had introduced himself, saying he'd heard Father was renovating, and that he, Frank, happened to be available. Obviously, being the recluse that he was, Father's only information about Frank had come from Frank himself.

I'd been hoping for neutral observer status, but was promptly drawn into a moral quandary on our very first day. Father's plan was for us to tear down the verandah in such a way as to save all the lumber for re-use on the extension. He instructed Frank and me to get a start on this demolition while he spent the morning buying additional building supplies. Since he still didn't trust me to do anything on my own, he also put me under Frank's authority.

As soon as Father was gone, Frank picked up a

sledge. "You take the far side, I'll take this one, what d'ya think?" he suggested.

I picked up a crowbar. "Okay," I agreed.

For the next hour, I didn't so much see Frank as hear him. He attacked the verandah like a whirling dervish. All you could hear was his smashing sledge, the splintering of wood, the shrieking of nails. I'm pretty sure Father had envisioned us starting from the roof, but Frank started from the bottom. Pretty soon there was very little holding anything up anymore.

"You don't think that's going to kind of . . . come down on its own?" I asked Frank during one of his rare five-second breaks. There were only two or three studs left supporting the verandah's entire top storey.

Frank looked up quizzically. "I guess we can only hope," he grinned. He picked up his sledge and resumed swinging.

Seconds later there was a loud crack. It was followed by a terrifying rending sound. Then, loud explosions as glass panes burst out of their buckling window frames. There was more splintering and screeching, and finally the whole structure tore slowly away, a two-storey accordion of wood and asbestos tile that left the rest of the house shuddering in a way no house ever should.

I was so astonished, I leaped clear barely in time.

"Hot Aunt Jemimah," Frank exclaimed happily. "Now we're cookin' with gas!"

The kitchen door to the verandah flew open and Mother almost stepped out into thin air.

"*Gott im Himmel,* what on earth happened!" she gasped. "Has anybody been hurt down there?"

"Nothing to worry about, Mrs. Niebuhr," Frank assured her cheerfully. "We're just taking down the verandah."

Mother looked like she was about to choke. We all gazed at the almost ten-foot-high heap of splintered wood and broken glass, with dust still swirling out of it. Finally Mother simply shook her head and slammed the door.

Frank must have registered some of her doubt. "Oh geez now, your dad said something about re-using the old lumber, didn't he?" he recalled. "I guess we should try and do a little salvaging, what d'ya think?"

That's what I thought we should do, and that's what we were doing when Father returned several hours later and practically dropped his drawers.

"What in the name of seventeen devils . . ." he blurted, but Mother had obviously been watching through the window and she hurried down. "Come in for lunch, Reinhard," she said quickly, gripping him firmly by the elbow. "Come on in; I have to talk to you."

They disappeared into the house, and they must have talked in the living room because I didn't hear anything from the kitchen. Mother brought out our lunch half an hour later, her face shut tight. By this time Frank was looking a bit uneasy—not least because we weren't finding an awful lot of salvageable lumber. "The thing is, you save a lot of time doing it this way," he insisted, not looking at our fast-growing scrap heap. "And time costs money, don't ya think?"

"So does lumber," I pointed out, knowing Father.

"Yeah but those studs are so old, they've turned rock-hard," Frank argued. "You try and pull a nail out of them—or bang one in, for that matter. Go ahead; you give it a try."

I tried, and he was right. The studs were like iron.

It saved Frank's bacon that day, because when Father came down after lunch I think he'd firmly decided that Frank had to go. But even after that, Frank couldn't stop being Frank. The next day Father caught him throwing topsoil into the plywood forms he'd just built for the addition's cement footings. "I dug them a bit too deep I guess," Frank explained, not stopping his energetic shovelling. "Gotta bring her up half a foot, maybe seven or eight inches, maybe ten, what d'ya think?"

"You can't use topsoil in a footing that's going to hold up a two-storey building," Father pointed out. "It'll compress and crack the cement. You have to use gravel—it's the code."

"Oh that's okay," Frank said. "I know the building inspector for this area. He won't give us any trouble."

Father looked nonplussed. "Frank, I'm building this addition for me."

Frank hesitated, then gave an embarrassed laugh.

On the third day, he cut twenty-four roof rafters to length without checking the accuracy of the piece he'd used as a guide. It turned out to be almost two feet short.

"Well okay, we can use them for the floor joists don't ya think?" he told Father hastily, hauling out his measuring tape. "What do we need, ten feet, twelve feet, maybe fourteen? There's enough there if it's . . . twelve."

"The addition's fifteen feet, Frank," Father said. He said it so quietly it sounded almost menacing.

✲

I wasn't there when Frank went home that night so I don't know who said what, but the next day, when we started working, Frank didn't show up.

"We'll build this extension on our own from now on," was all that Father said on the subject.

And that's what we did for the ten remaining days. We hadn't finished by the time Father went back to work, of course, so we had to buy a tarp to cover the roof, but luckily we had a very dry fall that year so nothing got wet. By Christmas, the roof was finished and the insulation was in, though the drywall hadn't been taped or painted, and the outside was still covered in tarpaper.

In fact, the outside of the house now looked worse than ever before—but at least the new addition showed undeniably that something was finally being done about it.

six

By the time Father had finished wiring and dry-walling the inside of our new addition, the fresh black tarpaper covering its exterior had begun to blanch and sag. The look that had once signalled "new enterprise" now suggested "abandoned initiative".

This was both true and untrue.

The fact was that city life had been ploughing through our family's cohesion like a bulldozer. On the farm we'd huddled together because everything had been new and unfamiliar. Father and Mother had been newly minted parents, we'd been new immigrants, and we'd all spoken the wrong language. As well, almost all our Mennonite church events had involved the whole family. We'd gone everywhere as a unit—to church, to town, to visit.

In Vancouver, this unity crumbled. Distances shrank, buses broke the family hammerlock on transportation, and, most important, the ratio of spies to strangers plummeted. In Agassiz, almost everyone had been a potential informant. In Vancouver, nobody cared.

The resulting freedom hit us like a blast of oxygen.

Mother joined several choirs, became backup church organist, taught German School on Saturdays, and made lots of new friends. Gutrun and Heidi went to separate schools, made separate friends, and began to explore separate interests. I didn't make a lot of friends but I discovered rock & roll, poetry, and the theatre. The issue of the house began to fade. For the first few years we'd all been intensely interested in having the house fixed up, but once we began to realize how long this might actually take, we set our sights on other goals.

Only Father remained essentially unchanged. By nature reserved, by inclination a hermit, he watched us scatter in all directions, looked thoughtful, shook his head—then picked up his tools and continued renovating.

It was sometime in the winter of my Grade Ten year that Grandfather Niebuhr died. Father took the train to Winnipeg to attend the funeral, but when he returned, it was at the wheel of a nicely preserved light brown 1955 Volkswagen beetle. This was an astounding turn of events, since I'm pretty sure even Father had had no idea he was inheriting a car when he'd left for the funeral. I'm not even sure he'd known that his father owned one. It wasn't the sort of thing the Niebuhrs talked about.

Nevertheless, there it was, a dilemma on wheels. Even I had to admit we didn't actually need a car in

Vancouver. Insurance was expensive, and there was a bus stop right in front of the house.

Father cancelled the insurance, parked the car in our back yard, and covered it with a tarp.

I poked and prodded, but I couldn't get either Father or Mother to divulge their plan. It's possible they didn't have one. I, on the other hand, did. I was fifteen, and my fondest fantasy was to own a '57 Chevy with twin stacks, a four-barrel carburetor and a 350 V8. But really, any kind of car would do. So even with a Beetle, this was a Cinderella story just waiting to happen, and I spent hours during class daydreaming about it.

On days when I didn't work after school, I raced straight home and made a bee-line for the dresser where Father kept the ignition key. At that time of the afternoon Mother was usually at church and my sisters were at friends' houses. I pulled off the tarp, settled into the driver's seat, inserted the key and fired it up.

The roar of the engine was the most satisfying sound I had ever heard.

I revved it. I idled it. I revved it, idled it, turned it off and turned it back on. Sometimes I dropped it into gear and drove the three car-lengths up to the house, then let it roll back down to our yard's back fence. Once I even popped the clutch and pulled an unexpected wheelie, almost hitting Father's new basement workshop. I imagined myself spinning off to school, arriving at the parking lot with everyone watching, the girls astonished, the boys jealous, the teachers impressed.

I spent so much time in that car that it soon ran out of gas. I had to buy a five-gallon canister of fuel at the B/A filling station on Fraser Street, lug it home through a series of back alleys, and hide it in the garden shed behind some leftover sacks of Portland cement.

"Why can't I drive our car?" I asked Mother again and again, because I didn't have the nerve to ask Father. "I'll pay for the insurance. With my own money. Honest!"

Mother gave me an odd look. "What money are you talking about?" she asked.

Eventually I heard them talking about it down in the basement, where Father was replacing all our lead pipes with copper. "He's got a perfectly good bicycle," Father pointed out. "It's safer and cheaper, and much more sensible. He's still a boy, Margarete. He'd just smash it up."

Mother murmured something I couldn't make out.

"I haven't seen any evidence of that," Father said. "I think he just wants to impress the girls—and he's much too young for that."

Mother's reply was inaudible.

"Since when?" Father demanded. "Well, maybe in Canada, but not in our family."

Of Mother's long reply, all I could catch were two words that sounded like "geraniums" and "waterspout".

"It could be," Father said. "But I'm not even sure about that. Maybe Bible college. I don't know. We'll have to see."

His pounding and scraping resumed.

That evening, I was doing homework in my curtained-off area of the new addition when Mother came in and sat down on my cot. "Good news," she said with a determined sort of brightness. "Father says that in about two weeks' time he'll have the two front bedrooms painted. Then we'll take the left one and you can have the right. They'll still need baseboards and a wardrobe, but that will have to wait until he's finished this addition for the girls. Isn't that wonderful?"

"That's great," I said. "But what about the car?"

Mother's expression wavered. "Don't push so hard," she said tiredly. "You know it never works when you push so hard."

"But it's so stupid!" I protested. "It's just sitting out there rusting, being wasted!"

"What's rusting?" Father asked. We hadn't heard him coming up the basement stairs. His head poked in between the curtains. His hair was plastered across his forehead and he had a smear of white paint across one cheek.

Mother got up and shouldered her way out. "It's like living between two rhinos," she muttered as she headed down the hall. Then, louder: "Two rhinos, do you hear me?" And louder still: "Rhinos!"

seven

Charlotte Anderson was a short, slightly plump, curly-haired girl who sat behind me in French class. She insisted on being called Carle. We were both members of our school's Poetry Club, and we both thought The Platters were kind of neat. We were also part of a small group of students who actually used the school library to borrow books rather than just hanging around in it. I liked her because she didn't seem to care about being popular, and she didn't wear makeup or big hair even though she didn't belong to a church that considered makeup a sin. As far as I knew, she didn't belong to any church at all.

"What are Mennonites?" she asked me one day in the library. "I mean, do you guys do polygamy and stuff?"

I wasn't actually sure what polygamy was, but it sounded unlikely. Mennonites didn't do much of anything that was any fun. In fact, all I could really explain about Mennonites was a long list of things we didn't do. No dancing, no TV, no movies, no drinking, no card-playing, no rock & roll—and then there were the Amish Mennonites who didn't even allow electricity, telephones, fancy clothes, jewellery, cars, and if you had a tractor, rubber tires.

Carle seemed impressed. "Wow. How do you guys ever manage to have any kids?"

It was a good question—and a conversational direction that made me feel nervous and fascinated.

On another occasion she asked, "What would happen if a Mennonite person did stuff that was on your list? You know, all that stuff you guys don't do? Would they, you know, excommunicate you or something?"

I didn't know what that meant either, but I doubted it. "I think they'd just kick you out of church."

"Excommunication," she said slowly, as if feeling out the syllables with her tongue. "Wow. Sounds heavy, doesn't it? I'll have to look that up."

And she must have, because a few days later she brought it up again. "Hey, Catholics do it too," she announced. "Mostly to writers and priests. For preaching heresies and stuff."

"The Mennonites don't like writers either," I agreed. "Writers make things up, which the church considers lying."

"But you want to be a writer," she pointed out. "What about that?"

"My parents don't know," I shrugged. "I don't talk about it."

"Wow," Carle said. "You know, it's almost like you're not even living in Canada." The next day she invited me to the Ladies Choice Valentine's Dance in our high school gymnasium, even though I couldn't dance.

During the following weeks, it became increasingly clear that Carle had decided I had to be well and properly patriated. It was her own little Canada Immigration Program, and she wasn't about to be discouraged by either my social clumsiness or my incredibly strict parents. "Phone me," she said when we parted in front of her house after I'd walked her home. "About 7 or 8 o'clock. Pretend you can't live without me."

"I can't phone you," I pointed out. "Our phone is right in the kitchen."

"Why would I care where your phone is?"

"You know what I mean," I said.

That night I traced the telephone line into our house, and discovered where it connected to our phone. It was at a little porcelain connection block with four metal clamps, but only three were being used. Each clamp was colour-coded. It looked pretty straightforward.

A few days later I found an old phone in a house that was being torn down several blocks from our place. It was an ancient wall model, still attached to the wall but with its wires cut and dangling. I found a similar connection block in the basement and scavenged the wire that led from it to the phone upstairs. I wrapped the phone and wire in my jacket and hurried home.

First thing I had to do was find out whether this phone even worked. Down in our basement I set it up beside our connection block and nervously began to hook its wires, one by one, to our clamps.

Red to red.

No reaction.

Yellow to yellow.

No reaction.

Suddenly it occurred to me that I actually had no idea what I was doing. Would trying to connect this phone to our house system maybe wreck our own phone? Could I possibly electrocute myself in the process?

I gingerly touched the remaining black wire to the black connector.

A loud crackling exploded from the handset. I yanked back my hand.

Oh shit oh shit oh shit.

I rushed upstairs and lifted the handset on our family phone.

The sweet sound of an ordinary dial tone flooded my ear. Praise God From Whom All Blessings Flow.

I hastened back down to the connection block.

Touch black wire to black connector. More terrifying crackling. I hesitated, then pushed more firmly on the connection. The crackling stopped.

Then, the faint but unmistakable sound of another normal dial tone.

Hot Aunt Jemimah!

Crouched down in my family's basement, flushed and triumphant, I felt as if I'd just made my very own direct connection with the modern world.

Besides, nobody I knew at school had their own phone.

Now the only problem left was how to keep this fact hidden from the rest of my family. I ended up concealing the wires behind the heating pipe that led from the nearby furnace up into my new bedroom at the front of the house. Then I moved my dresser next to the heating vent, so I could surreptitiously run the wire behind it and through a hole in its back, directly into the dresser's top drawer. It was tricky because this phone had been designed to hang on a wall, not lie flat under a heap of socks and T-shirts, but I solved that by taping the handset to the phone body with masking tape. It meant I'd have to pull off the tape every time I wanted to use it, and tape it up again when I was finished, but who cared.

My triumph almost ended in disaster just before supper when someone from church called my mother and both phones rang. Fortunately Father was in the basement and Mother and I in the kitchen, but even with my phone muffled by clothes and a closed bedroom door, its faint rings produced enough of a stereophonic effect that Mother looked momentarily puzzled. I hurried into my bedroom for an emergency disconnect, and after supper I took the back off my phone to see what could be done. It turned out to be easy; I simply disconnected the wire that powered the bell.

"You sound like you're a million miles away," Carle complained when I made my first call to her that evening.

I explained about the new phone and its unorthodox location.

"In your underwear drawer?" she demanded, giggling in a way that always made me break out in a sweat. "Oh wow; this I've absolutely got to see."

eight

My parents rarely went out together—and if they did, it was only on Sundays.

The limiting factor was Father. Regular weekdays were off limits because he worked on those days. Weekday evenings and Saturdays were off limits because those were Father's prime renovating times. Sunday mornings and evenings were taken up with church, and on Sunday afternoons Father liked to nap, which was fine because you couldn't work on Sundays anyway.

There were exceptions, but they were rare. Now and then Father had to give up a weekday evening to attend a men-only Church Administrative Meeting, where important congregational issues were discussed and voted on.

And then there were weddings.

It drove Father crazy that weddings always happened on a Saturday. It also didn't help that Mennonites had a lot of weddings, and we had a lot of relatives. Mother and the girls always seemed to be heading off to a wedding, for which they'd practiced musical pieces or memorized poems.

I disliked weddings almost as much as Father. It was one of the rare things we had in common. Neither of us had a knack for easy socializing. So the weddings of second or third cousins were automatically out. Even first cousins had to be pretty special to overcome our natural reluctance. But on this particular Saturday my Onkel Otto—Mother's brother—was getting married. His wife had died a few years earlier, and he was, as Onkel Jacob put it, "giving it another shot".

I could tell from the set of Mother's jaw that we didn't have a hope this time. This was her favorite brother, and a popular minister of the Ebenezer Mennonite Church in Chilliwack. Everyone who was anyone would be there. Mother said she had absolutely no intention of appearing at this wedding in her usual guise as a "grass widow".

So Father threw in the towel, but I got a lucky break. A week before the wedding, Mr. Meier at the Fraser Book & Record Company asked me if I could work the following Saturday.

Even Mother couldn't argue with that one. Paid work always took priority in our household. My parents considered debt a kind of unofficial sin, and we were still carrying a mortgage. Every extra nickel went toward paying it down.

Unbeknownst to Mr. Meier, his offer came with a special bonus. Chilliwack was far out in the Fraser Valley, and the wedding would go on well into the night. My parents would have to stay overnight in Chilliwack, then attend church there the next morning. They wouldn't be home until Sunday evening.

The implication wasn't lost on my parents. As they climbed into an Onkel's car for the ride to Chilliwack the following Saturday morning, Father warned me not to leave on any lights after I'd gone to bed, and not to fool around with any of his tools. Mother reminded me several times about the three pre-cooked meals she had stored in the fridge. My sisters gave me jealous looks.

Even Carle had recognized this arrangement's advantages when I'd told her about the wedding. "Hey, you can finally show me where you hide that illegal phone!" she enthused. "What time will you be home from work on Saturday?"

My knee jerk reaction was alarm. "Aw, you know, our place is still . . . you know . . . kind of . . . under construction . . ."

"Don't be silly, silly," she said. "You told me all about that. Why would I care what shape your house is in?"

But when she rang our doorbell on Saturday evening just after 7pm, she looked almost as nervous as me.

"Hi!" she said brightly. "Pizza delivery!" She really was holding a pizza. "I figured you might be starving so I picked this up along the way."

She was wearing a loose black V-neck sweater, black jeans, and a pair of those sandals that look like they've been made out of old rubber tires. Her blond hair was usually pulled back tightly in a long pony-tail, but not this time.

"Don't mind me," she said. "I had to tell my mom I was going to a tennis tournament. Sometimes I play at the Fraserview Racquet Club on weekend evenings."

I couldn't get over how different she looked. She seemed years older somehow, not like school at all, but I couldn't figure out why. The sandals, certainly; the hair, maybe—or maybe it had nothing to do with her clothes at all.

"Um . . . standing out here is nice, but it could get boring," she said. "And this pizza's getting cold. Are you going to invite me in or anything?"

I hastily stepped aside.

In the kitchen, I set out plates and cutlery, and we sat down to eat. I think the unexpected domesticity made us both feel awkward. She talked about her family and her tennis and something about accounting and typing courses, but I couldn't seem to keep my mind on the conversation. I just grunted and nodded a lot.

Things got a bit better when she asked if she could explore the house, and I got up to follow her around. She was really curious, and seemed fascinated by all the photographs of our huge extended family in the living room—especially the one portraying several hundred stiffly erect adults lined up in five ascending rows against the backdrop of an ornate mansion, with almost as many kids sitting or crouched or sprawled in two additional rows across the front. There were even some women in nuns' habits in the back row, which I couldn't explain.

"Wow—Mennonites must have about a thousand kids each," she laughed, gazing inquisitively from face to face. "So what happened about that in your family?"

I couldn't explain that either.

"And those huge estates," she marvelled. "That was in Germany?"

"West Prussia," I said. "But the Russians chased everyone out. In the war. Now it's all Poland."

She was amazed at Father's workshop, with its hundreds of tools hanging neatly along the walls, each tool outlined in black felt pen so you could always tell if anything was missing. The shop was spotlessly clean, but you could see that it was used for serious work because there were all sorts of glued and clamped furniture parts lying on the counters, and the bins were full of sawdust and bits of scrap wood. She gazed at it all for a long time from the doorway. "Scary," was all she said about it.

Back in our living room I demonstrated Father's stereo with my badly worn and scratched 45 RPM copy of Elvis' Jailhouse Rock, cranking the volume recklessly up to #8. The music exploded out of the speakers with such force that the glass vase on the window sill shook, and I hastily reached for the volume knob. "No, no, leave it up!" Carle shouted, and started doing The Twist. She was amazingly good, contorting her body so naturally and effortlessly that I despaired once again of ever being able to join the ranks of The English in any convincing way.

"Come on!" she yelled. "You can do it! Don't think so much; just jump in!" She grabbed my hand and pulled me into the middle of the living room floor, shoving the coffee table over for more room. I forced myself to stop worrying about how we were scuffing up Mother's waxed floor, or if the neighbours were being blasted out of their houses, and tried clumsily to imitate her. I don't think I did very well, but Carle insisted otherwise, and

I did kind of get into the groove eventually. We played that record about half a dozen times.

Finally she called a halt, and I shut off the record player. We flopped onto the sofa and mopped our faces with a dish towel. She asked for a glass of water, and I got it for her. She looked absolutely gorgeous, with her hair all tousled like that and her face all flushed. I just wanted to grab her and kiss her till we were out of breath, but I didn't have the nerve, so I just gazed at her in what I hoped wasn't an overly dopey way.

"I haven't seen your phone!" she exclaimed, jumping back up. "Your secret, illegal, criminal phone." We went back up the hall to the front of the house, where I showed her into my bedroom, which still wasn't quite finished, but I'd convinced Father I could easily move the furniture away from the walls whenever he got around to installing the baseboards. As for the missing closet doors, I didn't care.

She looked around thoughtfully, at the stacks of paperback books, the ivory chess set on the bureau, the typewriter sitting on the desk with the million cubbyholes I'd dragged home from a second-hand store on Fraser Street, and my bed with the lavishly decorated quilt covering a huge old-country duvet.

"Do you always keep your room this neat?" she demanded.

I admitted that I did.

"You're almost as bad as your dad," she joked, poking me with her elbow. "We're gonna have to work on that."

I liked the sound of that a lot.

She swivelled and sat down on my bed in a single

motion, patting the spot beside her. "Come and sit down with me," she said. "I want to talk to you."

I sat.

There was a pause, while she rubbed her hands on her knees and pursed her lips. Finally she took a deep breath and looked at me very directly. "You probably don't realize it," she said gently, "but you've really been staring at me a lot, lately. Especially here at your house, but at school too.

"No, no, I'm not trying to make you feel bad!" she protested as a wave of chagrin flooded over me. "I mean, I take it as a compliment; I know you're not trying to embarrass me. I think you've just been so . . . I don't know . . . locked up in your strict Mennonite life that sometimes you act as if you're kind of like . . . from another planet."

Only the fact that there wasn't a trace of accusation in her voice kept me from sinking right through the floor. That and the fact that I was utterly fascinated by what she was saying.

"Have you ever had a girlfriend before, Peter?"

I hesitated.

Carle looked at me almost sternly.

"No," I admitted.

"I thought so," she said. "And you've probably never even seen a girl's bare body before, right?"

I was having some trouble breathing.

"It's really not that big a deal," she said. "Look."

She took hold of the bottom of her sweater and pulled it up over her head, exposing a shiny white brassiere that covered her breasts almost completely. She undid a snap between the two cups and pulled the brassiere away.

Her breasts were small, but nicely round and firm-looking, with dark nipples and a red line under each one that must have resulted from her tight bra. They looked to me both deliciously exotic and utterly innocent somehow.

I wanted immediately to palm them. Instead, I lunged for the bedroom door and pulled it closed.

Carle laughed. "There's nobody home, you dummy," she said. "Don't be so nervous. And anyway, my very best feature is my legs. Wanna see?"

She tugged down her jeans and lay across the bed on her side, letting the light from the window fall more directly onto her legs.

They certainly looked like very nice legs to me, what with being both female and at closer range than I'd ever seen them before.

"Oh well, I guess you're a boob guy," Carle said resignedly. "Most guys are, I'm told. Too bad for me, I guess." She rolled onto her back, her breasts thrusting up enticingly.

"No, no," I protested. "Your breasts are beautiful. Really. I mean, you're really beautiful." And I meant it too.

She seemed pleased. "Aw shucks," she mocked. She wriggled closer. "You can touch them if you want."

That seemed like a marvellous idea.

It was an amazing experience. They were so very unlike any part of the male body; smooth, firm, yet soft too. I cupped them eagerly, enjoying the feel against my palms, squeezing a little. Carle didn't move, but I saw her eyes close. On impulse, I buried my head against her chest and rubbed my nose against her nipples.

She made a small sound in her throat and wrapped an arm around the back of my head. I found myself instinctively taking a nipple between my lips and sucking gently. She didn't seem to mind. I sucked a little harder, and she made that sound again, and clutched my head more tightly. But then I got carried away and pressed her nipple too hard against my teeth with my tongue and she abruptly pulled away. "Hey, no biting!" she protested.

I apologized abjectly.

She sat up and shook out her tousled hair. "That's okay, don't worry about it. Besides, it's your turn now. Let's see what your best features are."

That notion hadn't occurred to me, but I could see the logic. She was sitting near-naked on my bed, and I was still fully dressed. So I took off my shirt, then my jeans, and I was just pulling off my socks when we suddenly heard voices in the stairwell outside, and a rattling of keys.

We looked at each other in horror.

"Shit!" I breathed.

"Your parents?" Carle hissed. "But I thought . . ."

"The wedding must have ended early," I blurted. "And the first thing they're gonna do is come in here."

"Where can I hide?" She was frantically pulling on her jeans.

There wasn't any place to hide. The closet had no doors. The rest of my furniture was too low.

"This opens," I urged, pushing up the street-side window. "Jump out through here."

"You've got to be kidding!"

"It's only a four-foot drop. And you'll land behind a bush."

"That better be true, mister." She turned, clutching her sweater and brassiere to her chest. Then, with impressive agility, she swung through the window and dropped out of sight. I slammed down the window and lunged under the covers just as my bedroom doorknob turned and the door opened.

"What? Still awake, and all the lights on?" Father demanded. He stuck his head in all the way and looked around suspiciously the way he always did, but I could tell that he was in a good mood because he said it without his usual irritation. I guessed the shortened wedding had something to do with that.

Mother's face appeared above Father's shoulder, and the girls' heads appeared under his arms. "Did you have a good time without us?" Gutrun asked. "Whose shoes are those?" Heidi demanded. "Was there enough to eat in the fridge?" Mother wanted to know.

"The food was delicious," I assured Mother. "I was just reading a bit before going to sleep. How was the wedding?"

Father disappeared, leaving the womenfolk to chatter. "It was alright," Mother said. "We played those two Mozart pieces and Gutrun performed the Bach minuet. Onkel Jacob made a fool of himself at the after-wedding with something he called a "toast"— apparently the English do this all the time, but I never did understand what bread has to do with it. But Lisbeth's family did a short skit that had everyone howling."

"I want to know whose shoes those are," Heidi insisted.

"Go to bed, Heidi," I said. "Mother, why was the wedding so short?"

"Yes, off to bed with you two," Mother agreed, shooshing the girls away. "And don't forget to brush your teeth." She turned back to me. "Well, Walter had to get back to Vancouver for church tomorrow, and no one else had enough room in their cars. So we really didn't have any choice. Your father was delighted, of course. We missed at least half the after-wedding."

"Why doesn't anybody ever listen to me?" I could hear Heidi whining in the bathroom.

Gutrun made a muffled reply.

"Well, I'm off to bed too," Mother said. "Did you enjoy the peace and quiet?"

"Yes I did, Mother. Good night."

"Good night, son." Mother crossed the hall into their bedroom, leaving my bedroom door open. I could never figure out why. Father always did that too.

I could still hear the girls talking in the kitchen. "What shoes?"

"Those shoes in Peter's room."

"They're Peter's of course."

"No they weren't."

"Who else's would they be?"

"They weren't Peter's," Heidi insisted.

"Heidi, you're such a fussbudget."

"I am not!"

"Are too!"

"Am not!!"

I closed my bedroom door.

Below my bedroom window I could just make out the top of Carle's head behind the mulberry bush. "Are you still there?"

Her face turned up at me. "Where else would I be in my bare feet? Throw down my socks and shoes."

"Sorry it took so long. Everybody was talking."

I could hear her snort. "That's okay. I had a nice talk with a passing raccoon. And a tomcat."

"With a what?"

"A raccoon."

"Oh. Yeah, there is one. He mostly lives in that tree. Here's your shoes. I pushed the socks inside."

Carle bent down to put them on and then turned back up to fix me with a look so stern that I could make it out clearly even in the gloom. "Peter Niebuhr, if I ever so much as hear a whisper about tonight from anyone—and I mean any single person in the entire universe—I'll absolutely kill you. I really truly mean it. You promise?"

"I promise."

"Cross your heart and hope to die a grisly death by torture and hanging and having your nose cut off?"

"Cross my heart," I assured her.

"Alright then." She stepped out from behind the bush and slipped across the lawn. Suddenly she stopped, turned and came back a few steps. "And next time, you really will have to show me your stupid phone!"

She grinned and was gone.

nine

On Saturday, May 15, 1965, just a month before my high school graduation, Mother died in a car crash on the freeway.

She and my sisters had been on their way to another wedding in Chilliwack, having caught a ride with a distantly related nurse. The nurse had just worked a double shift, and the rooftop drumming of the rain, which had been falling all day, had apparently lulled her to sleep. The car smashed into a power pole at full highway speed.

I was at work at the Fraser Book and Records Company when Elder Wiebe arrived with the news. When I saw him enter the front door, I merely thought of him as a special, exalted customer. When he strode through the length of the store without looking at any of the merchandise, I decided something important must have happened. When he conferred in a low voice with Mr. Meier in his office, I assumed the important matter was probably something bad. When he stepped out of Mr. Meier's office and they both came directly to my cubicle in the back, my stomach sank.

"My son," Elder Wiebe said gravely, putting his hand on my shoulder in an adult way that sharply increased my alarm. "You are going to have to be very strong." I could see Mr. Meier's face over his shoulder, looking sick.

I have no idea how long Elder Wiebe talked to me. I don't really remember anything he said. What I gleaned was that Mother was dead, and that both Heidi and Gutrun were hurt but alive in the Chilliwack General Hospital. There was also something about Father, but by then I was already running out the door. I think somebody ran after me for about a block, but I can't be sure.

I was still half a block from home when I heard Father's wailing. Maybe the front door was open, maybe one of the windows. When I got inside there were people standing and kneeling, but all I saw was Father writhing on the living room floor. His face was an appalling shade of purple and his mouth was making the most horrible animal noises. I threw myself on top of him and tried to hold him, but he thrashed me off. I don't think he knew what he was doing.

Mother's death was the worst possible thing that could have happened to our family. I suppose that sounds obvious, but Mother was the glue that had always held our family together. She'd functioned as buffer and interpreter between Father and me, and as an intermediary between Father and the rest of the Mennonite community. She'd also just begun to teach my sisters to become women. Gutrun was only fourteen, Heidi twelve.

Besides that, it seemed enormously unfair to Mother herself. After years of working alongside Father, dawn till dusk, uncomplaining, resolute, she had finally begun to taste the kind of life she'd always dreamed of—filled with music, friends, a little leisure. I myself had just been getting to know her. We'd joined the same chamber choir, had begun to have serious talks.

All of this washed away in an instant.

It bothered me for years that we'd parted unhappily. I'd agreed to come to that wedding, had even rehearsed some music with her, but when Mr. Meier called to tell me I could work that Saturday, I once again chose the work. I think Mother felt betrayed, though she didn't say much. I made it worse with some flip remark about weddings in her family being a dime a dozen and what was the big deal.

When the nurse drove up, Mother climbed into the front passenger seat. Ordinarily, that would have been my seat. I was prone to car-sickness, and sitting in the back seat always made me throw up. I guess if I'd honoured my promise to attend that wedding, I might have been the one who was killed.

I've never known what to do with that realization.

I can't remember who stayed at our house to look after Father while Onkel Jacob drove me to the Chilliwack Hospital to see my sisters. When we got there, he parked, but made no move to get out. "I'm no good at this sort of thing," he apologized. "Hospitals scare the dickens out of me."

I found my sisters lying in adjacent beds, still hooked up to various medical machines. Gutrun had her left arm in a sling and cuts all over her face and arms. Heidi's head was bandaged and she had a lot of cuts as well. They were enormously relieved to see me because, despite their pleas and arguments, the nurses hadn't let them go see Mother, who was apparently recovering in a different part of the hospital.

I took too long trying to figure out what to say about that.

Gutrun's eyes grew huge. "No," she whispered desperately. "No. No. No."

Heidi looked frantically at Gutrun and then at me. "What?" she demanded. "What? Is Mother . . . isn't Mother . . ." An alarmed nurse, attracted by her cries, poked in her head and then quickly closed the door.

We spent the next hour huddled together on Heidi's bed, the girls unable to stop crying, me still numbly dry-eyed, patting and hugging them helplessly.

I navigated the following week like a sleepwalker. Father had gone from hysterical to comatose, so everyone turned to me. Apparently, I dealt with the doctors, handled insurance matters, and arranged for Mother's death certificate. I hired the undertaker, filled out official forms, met with the necessary bureaucrats and organized Mother's funeral. I don't remember any of it.

All I recall of the funeral is my surprise when I entered the church and found it crammed to the rafters. I'd had no idea that Mother had so many friends. When the service was over and we were driving to the cemetery, I looked back and saw the line of cars with their headlights on stretching all the way from Marine Drive to the top of the hill at Fraser and 57th Avenue—a distance of well over a mile. More cars with lit headlights were still coming over the hill when we turned east on Marine Drive and I lost sight of them.

It rained during the entire burial service, and everyone seemed to be crying except me. It wasn't until I fled to the movie theatre at Fraser and 43rd Avenue three days later to watch whatever was showing that I was able to let go. The story, about a naïve boxer who is set up only to be slapped back down by a clutch of human vultures, struck me as so utterly tragic that I couldn't stop crying. I watched it four times in a row without ever getting up, until the end of the last showing at midnight. It was called "The Harder They Fall", starring Humphrey Bogart.

I walked the streets for the rest of the night, still crying. I couldn't seem to stop. Once I went into an all-night restaurant for half an hour to warm up, but the waitress kept asking me what was wrong, so I left. When I finally got home at six o'clock in the morning, I crawled into bed without taking off my clothes, and slept until late in the afternoon. I don't think anyone even noticed.

ten

Several weeks after the funeral, once he'd recovered a little, Father called a family council.

He looked gaunt and exhausted, with that defeated expression back on his face. His voice was hoarse and low.

"I've been thinking about this," he said. "Now that your mother's gone, I'm going to have to be both your father and mother. So I want you all to start thinking about me that way."

We must have looked puzzled—in my case, somewhat alarmed.

"The confidences, the things you used to tell Mother instead of me," he said. "Your secrets. I need to know them so I can help."

Gutrun looked apprehensive, Heidi perplexed.

"With what?" I asked.

"Your upbringing," Father said. "I know that Mother did most of the child-raising, but she's gone now so

I'm going to have to do it. And to do it I need you to confide in me. Gutrun, how about you first?"

Gutrun was now looking decidedly flustered. "I . . . I don't know what . . . what do you want me to say, Father?"

Father looked uncertain. "Well, whatever you . . . whatever you used to tell Mother. About . . . everything."

Gutrun seemed stumped, and Heidi still perplexed. I was trying frantically to think up something to say.

"Peter?"

I hadn't had enough time. I shrugged. "Actually I didn't . . . Mother and I never really talked all that much . . ."

Father sighed. "How about you, Heidi?"

Heidi looked around the circle, visibly distressed, then abruptly burst into tears. "Oh I really, really wish Mother hadn't died," she sobbed. She clutched at a cushion and buried her face into it.

Father's face began to crumple, and tears rolled down his cheeks. Gutrun stiffened her jaw valiantly but couldn't hold back a flood of tears. I felt a stinging pressure against my eyeballs and a deep helplessness in my chest. I yanked myself off the sofa and fled.

During the following weeks, Father began assembling a shrine to Mother in the living room. There was no Mennonite tradition for this, so at first we didn't realize what he was doing. He used the top of the two speaker cabinets. He set up photos of Mother that he'd pulled out of our family albums, arranged some of her brooches and necklaces around them, and her favourite scarf. There was a notebook with some of her handwritten poems. No one was allowed to touch or move any of these things, and he spent many an hour, late at night after the evening's renovating, just sitting on the sofa staring at them. Whenever I came in from a concert or reading or a date with Carle I'd find him there, his nose red, his face wet. Sometimes he didn't even look up.

Various aunts showed up, sent or motivated by the church, or our relatives, or their own concern over Gutrun's and Heidi's welfare. They meant well, but generally stayed only a few weeks. Father tolerated but never encouraged them, and adamantly refused to let them touch Mother's clothes or any of her other possessions. Since each of the aunts tended to assert her own vision about what was right or wrong for a young girl to do, the girls found these "invasions of mercy," as Onkel Jacob called them, increasingly frustrating. Eventually Father put a stop to them.

While I managed for the most part to stay clear of all this, it made the climate at home so unpredictable that I began to hang around Carle's place a lot more. We had, in the meantime, graduated together, and were planning to enroll at the same university. She was going to study History and I was going to take Creative Writing. Her parents proved to be astonishingly easy-going and sympathetic, even letting me sleep over in their basement whenever Carle insisted it was too late at night or too emotionally corroding for me to go back to my own home. It gave me something like an alternative home, and Carle the perfect opportunity to complete her home-grown Canada Immigration Program, for which she now had my complete and enthusiastic cooperation. Whenever she could—when her parents were in bed after a boozy party or a dinner with lots of wine—she snuck down to the rec-room where I was sleeping on the couch and slipped into my sleeping bag, waking me with fondlings and kisses that I quickly learned to return in equal measure. She seemed a miracle in every sense of the word, and though I sometimes felt guilty about the fact that these lessons in Canadian citizenship were probably due at least in part to everyone's sympathy for a motherless boy, I was still quite willing to take advantage of it. I was, finally, gaining access to the world of the English, and a whole new, tantalizing future.

Whenever Father asked me where I'd been when I missed a night at home, I said I'd overnighted at Carl's place. Carl Anderson quickly became a school-chum, chess partner, soccer team-mate and constant companion. I mentioned him so often that it wasn't long before he'd taken on a fairly well-defined reality in my life. Father didn't seem to notice his invisibility, or more likely wasn't interested. Carl was, after all, an Englisher.

Nevertheless, there was a fair amount of uproar the evening the phone rang during supper, and Father answered it. "*Ja?*" He listened for a moment. "*Was?* Who you vill speaking?"

He listened again, his brow becoming furrowed. "Peter? *Ja? Und wer ist es* speaking, pleeze?"

I was already reaching urgently for the receiver. I couldn't imagine who would be calling me at home, and didn't like the sound of what I was hearing. But Father refused to relinquish the phone.

"Vat? You is be Carl? Carl Anderson? *Wie bitte*?"

When he finally handed me the receiver, his look was alarmed. "This Carl person is a girl?" he demanded.

I grabbed the phone. "Hello?"

"Aw jeez," Carle apologized. "I didn't think your dad ever answered the phone. I thought you'd be picking up your criminal phone. Did I screw up by calling?"

"Oh hello . . . Charlotte," I said lamely, turning away from Father. "What's . . . what's up?"

"Oh shit I have, haven't I?" Carle sounded truly appalled. "Hey, I'm really, really sorry. Make something up quick—you're a writer. Tell him I'm your parole officer. Or how about—never mind. I shouldn't be joking about this, should I?"

"No," I said. "That's true. We're in the middle of supper just now. Can I call you back?"

"This is such a bummer," Carle groaned. "I don't know what I was thinking."

"Oh don't worry, it's quite all right," I said. "I'm sure we can take care of it in the morning. I'll talk to you then, okay? Goodbye."

As I hung up I was still desperately trying to tie up the loose ends of a sufficiently coherent story to get myself out of this mess, but one look at Father, and then at my astonished, suddenly enlightened sisters, and I saw I was sunk. Father seemed more stunned than angry at the enormity of my deceit.

"What I just want to know," he said finally, after a

long, painful silence during which nobody ate much of anything, "is where on earth you spent those nights when you claimed you were at this "Carl's" place."

I stared expressionlessly at my plate, and then sighed.

"I was just walking the streets," I said. "I went into all-night restaurants when it was cold." He still looked doubtful. "I couldn't stop thinking," I said, "about Mother."

When I told Carle the story the next afternoon, the two of us in her bed while her parents were at work, she whistled softly. "Boy, you are a writer," she said, languidly tracing her finger under my chin and down my neck and chest. "What a check-mate. You had him cold."

"Not my sisters, though," I said, tonguing her left breast and sliding my hand appreciatively over the enticing swell of her bum. "Maybe Heidi believed me, but I'm pretty sure Gutrun didn't. The look she gave me made me feel like a Judas."

"Judas who?"

"The guy who betrayed Christ."

"Whoa. Isn't that getting a bit heavy?"

"You're right," I said, and proceeded to pay a lot more attention to the matter at hand.

eleven

The summer following Mother's death, Father announced that his renovation of our living room, dining room, bathroom and kitchen was now complete.

Once again this came as a surprise, because we'd thought those rooms had been completed years ago. Not so, apparently. Minute changes had continued under our inattentive noses, but these were finally finished. The focus of Father's renovation plans would now revert to the front (Father's and my) bedrooms.

These too looked virtually completed. True, they still lacked baseboards and closet doors, but we'd been living without those for years. The drywall, wiring and windows had all been replaced. The walls had been painted. Still, they had remained on Father's list, from which nothing could hide—not even my illegal phone, which Father discovered when he pulled back my desk from the wall to install the baseboards.

"What's this?" he demanded when I got home.

I grimaced, mentally kicking myself for not having anticipated this.

"It's my extension phone."

Father looked nonplussed. "There was an extension phone in this house?"

"No, I installed it myself."

The shouting match that ensued began as an argument about the legality of the phone, but quickly broadened in scope. This was simply the latest example of my apparently inexorable slide into sin and abomination. The Englishers' influence on me had gone from alarming to catastrophic. By now my status as a Christian was in serious doubt, my salvation imperiled, and worst of all, if I continued down this path, I was becoming an impediment to Father's own salvation.

That brought the argument to an astonished halt.

Yes, absolutely, Father insisted. If he couldn't give a convincing accounting of himself at the Gates of Heaven when his time was up, those gates would remain closed to him. It stood to reason. A man unable to raise his own son to God-fearing adulthood would be in no position to expect entry into Paradise.

I found this theory highly suspect, and I said so. I also thought it an ingenious form of blackmail, but didn't say that because I didn't know the German word for it. I'd never been aware of the concept during my childhood.

On the other hand, over the next several months, I found myself considering Father's accusations in a more neutral way. Maybe he had a point. Maybe I wasn't being a good Christian. In fact, maybe—a formerly unthinkable thought—maybe I wasn't, and didn't want to be, a Christian at all.

At first encounter, the idea terrified me. Everything I was, and ever had been, was tied up in it. My history. My identity. My entire world had always been interpreted as Us versus Them. Now I was considering the possibility that I was no longer one of Us. It was as startling as suggesting I might not be human.

For years, I'd argued, challenged and rebelled. But I'd never considered defection.

I spent the rest of the summer working in a saw mill and, when university started, I left home and moved into a dingy little basement room in the Marpole area. It was damp and buggy, but it was mine. To my amazement, Father let me insure and use the VW Beetle—not because he thought this was a good idea, but because he couldn't disagree that it was just sitting there rusting in our back yard, being wasted. Fifteen years of life in Canada, with its routinely wasteful ways, hadn't changed Father's attitude on this subject in the least.

I began to write in earnest. Poems just seemed to pour out of me. Often, I wrote half a dozen poems a day. My little room filled up and then began to bulge with papers, books, manuscripts, journals. Making love to Carle in my narrow bed became dangerous, our enthusiastic thrashing invariably bringing down showers of books. Space became so tight that I took to writing longhand in the bathtub, and typing up manuscripts on a huge old portable that straddled the bathroom sink. It was a total mess—and utterly exhilarating.

I went home less and less often. I felt badly for abandoning the girls, but the freedom proved irresistible. And I was rapidly building a new family, mostly other writers, artists, actors—people who accepted me, encouraged me—people who defined themselves by things they did rather than by what they didn't do.

I wrote day and night. I don't know when I slept. There were parties, readings, book launches, sit-ins, demonstrations, be-ins, even riots, and I attended many of those, but soon discovered that writing and being wrecked didn't mesh. Neither did my past and my future. It was as if I'd boarded a rocket-ship to another planet, and was leaving a long trail of abandoned family, relatives, friends, goals, dreams and possessions in my wake.

The jettisoning was continual—mostly voluntary, sometimes not. I swapped church for a lively readers' club. I abandoned choir practice and joined a political discussion group. I cancelled my flute lessons and took up sky-diving and motorcycling. I'd been writing in both German and English, and now I dropped the German.

Even Father's VW Beetle finally fell victim to this process. As I was driving to classes one Wednesday morning, crossing 14th Avenue at Waterloo, I caught a glimpse of an approaching chromed radiator out of the corner of my eye, just before the big blue Lincoln Town Sedan smashed into my front passenger side. My driver's side door sprang open, flinging me unconscious onto the pavement, still clutching the broken steering wheel.

I regained consciousness just long enough to hear a hysterical woman's voice sobbing "Ohgod ohgod ohgod, is he dead?" and then, in a rising wail: "But I was only taking my books to the library!"

I was taken to the Emergency Ward at St. Paul's Hospital, where I was treated for a concussion and various cuts and bruises. They stitched me up, and I phoned Carle. She wasn't home, but her mother took the message. Carle showed up several hours later and took me to her place, where she could fuss over me more efficiently. The nurses had suggested waking me every few hours during any sleeping episodes, to check if I'd gone into a coma, and Carle did this conscientiously, in ways the nurses probably hadn't envisioned.

I decided not to tell Father about the accident until I'd gotten a ruling from the Insurance Bureau, but when I dropped in for a brief visit a few days later, Gutrun said Father already knew all about it. I assumed, from her accusing undertone, that she felt I should have told Father immediately, but that wasn't it at all. It turned out the ambulance crew had gone through my wallet while I was unconscious, and called the number listed under "In case of emergency". I'd completely forgotten that Father was still listed on my ID papers as next of kin.

Father, with his limited English, had understood only enough to imagine the worst, and had immediately hurried off to St. Paul's Hospital. But there'd been a bus strike on, so Father had cancelled work and walked the entire ten miles to the hospital, only to be told that I'd just left in the company of a young woman. Since he assumed that I'd asked for him to be called in the first place, my thoughtless departure, leaving no explanatory message, struck him as the height of disrespect. He'd walked home in a rage, and was still in no mood to accept either my explanation or apology. During our entire discussion of the subject, he never once stopped dipping and applying his paint roller, up and down, up and down, spreading primer on the recently filled and sanded walls of the breakfast nook.

My first book—a collection of poems—was published in 1969. It was a lovely production, with hard-cover binding, letterpress printing and a full-color dust jacket. I immediately hurried over to Father's house to show it off.

My sisters exclaimed over it in a very gratifying way. Father seemed far more conflicted, and at first he said nothing at all.

He thumbed through the entire volume several times, back and forth, back and forth. I wasn't sure what he was looking for, because he didn't read English, and I'm not sure he knew either, but eventually his manner changed.

"You say this is a book of poems," he said. "But look at this . . . and this." He pointed to the empty spaces below a number of shorter poems, and the empty page between each section of poems. There were empty pages at the beginning and the end of the book as well, and the title page contained only a single line. "You call this a book of poems, but it looks only half full to me," he pointed out. "This is only half a book of poems."

He handed it back to me and shook his head. "You're still trying to make it through life by taking short-cuts, Peter," he said. "And until you learn to stop cheating like this, you'll never amount to anything. I tell you this as a well-meaning father, whether you're prepared to accept it or not. I know we live in a country where shoddy work is considered acceptable, but remember this: God is not fooled. And God will be the final judge as to whether we have succeeded or failed in this life."

I looked directly into his eyes, something I couldn't remember having done in years, and it was the book in my hands that gave me the nerve to do it.

"May I ask you a question, Father?"

"Certainly."

I took a deep breath and held it for a moment, trying to keep the book in my hands from shaking.

"Am I, in any way . . . I mean, can you . . . even if only just a bit . . . can you . . . do you think you could ever accept me for who I am instead of . . . you know . . . instead of who you wanted me to be?"

Father didn't say anything for a long time. I think he was honestly considering the question.

But finally he shook his head. "No," he said sadly. "No, I can't do that, Peter. Because it isn't what I want you to be. It's what God wants you to be. What's right and what's wrong isn't negotiable that way. It's God's law, not mine."

And then he shrugged, helplessly. At least, it looked helpless to me.

twelve

For some years after I left home, Father and the girls changed rooms around the house like musical chairs. Sometimes this was to accommodate Father's ongoing renovations; sometimes it was to accommodate newer realities. When I'd moved out, Heidi had moved into my old front bedroom so both girls could have their own space. Then, as their social life increased, the girls took over both front bedrooms, for easier and less disruptive late-night access to the front door, while Father took over the girls' former bedroom in the back. When Gutrun left home, Heidi moved into Gutrun's bedroom because it was larger, and when Heidi left home, Father eventually installed doors in the closets of both front bedrooms—then closed their heating vents and shut them down. There was no point, after all, in heating rooms nobody was using. The breakfast nook, too, was mothballed shortly after it was finished the following year, because Father alone had no use for it either.

With fewer disruptions, Father's renovating began to show greater progress. Scaffolding finally sprouted up around the house exterior, and the next summer the limp and sagging tarpaper was renewed and the whole house enveloped in a layer of chicken wire. Stucco followed, and by that fall the house underwent its most visible transformation, if in an oddly 50's retro sort of way. Father's plans, conceived at least twenty years earlier, had made no concessions to subsequent developments in home color or design.

"Well, better late than never, I suppose," the infinitely patient Mr. Windebank remarked to me on one of my increasingly rare visits. "Would there be any chance of some landscaping, d'you think?"

There was, and over the next three years Father renovated the lawn, the garden, and buried some lengths of water pipe for a fountain, though he never got around to installing a pump. He even built a garage in the back, though he never owned another car.

Living alone stimulated ("aggravated," according to Onkel Jacob) Father's instincts for thrift and economy. He would walk for miles to save a nickel on a pound of potatoes. He bought size Large second-hand clothes at the Hospital Auxillary, which he made the girls re-tailor to fit his size Small frame. He wore four layers of clothes to reduce his heating bill. At some point he discovered that the gas company charged a monthly base rate regardless of actual gas consumption, so he calculated precisely how many minutes of gas consumption this base rate paid for, then kept a daily log to track his furnace usage—making sure he never used more than that tiny monthly allotment.

Not content with those results, and knowing that most of a house's heat is lost through its windows, Father fitted all the dining room and living room windows with thick Styrofoam inserts. This reduced the rooms to a sepulchral gloom, but utilized his precious daily minutes of gas consumption much more efficiently. He installed a small free-standing fireplace in the living room, to burn the increasing amounts of paper advertising and political propaganda that was being shoved through his mail slot.

Thus, on all but the coldest days of the year, his routine never varied. He made marine cabinets for a boatbuilding factory during the day, then renovated the house from the moment he got home until suppertime. After a brief meal, he renovated some more. At nine o'clock he downed tools, lit the furnace or fireplace, and spent a final hour just sitting in the living room, gazing forlornly at Mother's unchanging shrine.

He was lonely and depressed, and why wouldn't he have been? He'd worked like a steam thresher all his life, with precious little to show for it, and now his closest companion in the world was gone. Everyone agreed that life hadn't given him a fair shake. Onkel Jacob sometimes referred to Father as a *Pechvogel*—literally a "tar-bird," a bad-luck sign—which always instinctively raised my hackles, but which was hard to deny.

That said, even Onkel Jacob agreed that Father was no whiner. A cynic and a pessimist, yes; quick to judge and harsh in those judgements, but he rarely complained about his own fate. I sometimes saw him as a kind of Job, whom God was testing to the limits of his endurance. He may have seen himself that way too.

He made no effort to do anything about improving his social life, which deteriorated even further after the girls left home. Some people tried to convince him to marry again, but he refused to even consider the idea. To him, it would have been the worst kind of betrayal.

Eventually, only half-joking, I suggested a dog or a television set. But Heidi pointed out that Father wasn't a doggy sort of person, and Gutrun reminded me that Mennonites frowned on television-watching.

I reminded her that while I'd worked for the Fraser Book & Record Company, one of my jobs had been to help Mennonite customers camouflage the stereos and television sets they'd purchased from our store.

Yes, but this was Father we were talking about.

She had a point.

Nevertheless we tried, and to our surprise, Father didn't refuse outright. He said he'd think about it—and he did, for about a year. We kept on nudging and cajoling, and he finally gave in, though with clear provisos. It would only be a black & white TV, and he would only tune in to nature programs.

I questioned where one could still get a black & white TV these days, but Father said he'd already located one, at the Goodwill Store on Tenth Avenue, selling for twenty-five dollars.

A week later, when I dropped by, the TV was sitting on an old apple crate in the corner of the living room. I helped him hook it up.

At first, it seemed we'd struck pay dirt. Father enjoyed the nature shows. We could tell because, though he refused to make any changes to his renovating schedule, the 9pm to10pm slot became his entertainment hour, locked in as rigidly as everything else in his life. If anyone was visiting him at that hour, they had to watch his shows with him or leave.

But in time, Father's interest in nature programming waned. He began watching the late-night news instead, and this produced a dramatically different effect. Since he had never read newspapers, listened to the radio or paid much attention to world events, Father had no defenses against so much dispiriting information. He was truly shocked to discover the mess the world was in. It made him even more bitter, more judgemental, more convinced that the world had forfeited any right to much clemency in its relentless pursuit of ungodly ways. He began attending evangelical revival meetings, and listening to Bible-thumping sermons on a local German-language radio station. His Christian faith became even more tight-fisted, rule-based, and Old Testament than it had been before.

My relationship with him deteriorated almost in lock-step. We were soon at a point where I could barely make it inside his door before he began to preach at me like a radio evangelist. He simply couldn't accept that I had given up on Christianity. He was convinced that I simply hadn't yet understood the message. He seemed to think that if he repeated it a thousand times, I might finally grasp his point.

Because I certainly hadn't grasped it yet. While my sisters had gone on to marry God-fearing husbands and to raise Christian families, I was living in communes, smuggling hashish, participating in riots and botching my way through a string of common-law relationships. When I finally did settle down with a permanent life partner, we didn't bother getting married, so our children, according to Father, were bastards. He refused to have anything to do with them.

I thought we might have more to talk about after I built my own house with an attached four-storey round tower on a mountain-top in the Fraser Valley, but he found the design too unorthodox and the work too imprecise.

But the biggest boulder between us remained his salvation. He kept insisting that if I didn't rejoin the church, his salvation was forfeit. No amount of debate or discussion, by my sisters or anyone else, could convince him otherwise.

We never did resolve this issue.

And then, in the fall of 1993, Father cut his right index finger while building the basement cold-storage room that Mother had always wanted. It happened as he was cutting a piece of plywood on his table saw. No one else was there when it happened, and none of us were prepared for his reaction.

To us, Father had simply had a minor accident while renovating. A brief visit to the Emergency ward of Vancouver's General Hospital had dealt with the wound. But to Father, who had always been justly proud of his unscarred hands after sixty years of carpentry, it was a lethal sign. He was losing his touch, his equipment-operating reflexes, his woodworking instincts. From here on, it could only get worse.

He brooded about this for months. He worked more and more slowly, often stopping to stare for minutes at a time at nothing in particular. He was becoming so distracted that we really did begin to worry about just how safe it was for him to operate his shop machinery.

Finally he said he'd made up his mind. He was going to put his house on the market and apply for an apartment in a Mennonite senior citizens' complex.

But with provisos.

First, he would complete the renovating. He said he was almost finished anyway. And the purchasers, needless to say, would have to be people who truly appreciated the house, who would live in it and honor it for all the work and sweat he had put into it. A quarter of a century of our history was buried within its frame. He didn't care, he said, whether it took five months or five years to find that kind of buyer. He wasn't in any hurry.

And he wasn't, though he didn't have to wait five years. He didn't even have to wait five months. Within three weeks Father's realtor had found a buyer who spoke a little German, and who was delighted with the house and perfectly content to agree to Father's provisos. This man took an entire morning to peruse the house, responding enthusiastically to Father's detailed before-and-after descriptions of the house's features. He said he was happy to wait until Father's renovations were complete; indeed, he insisted on it. He and his family had only recently moved to BC from Ontario, he explained, and were renting their current house on a month-by-month basis. He told Father to take his time.

Father was delighted and relieved. For the first time in years, he looked almost happy again. He actually hummed to himself as he installed the final drywall in the stairwell to the basement, and brought his tape-recorder into his bedroom so he could listen to sermons while he painted the last unpainted upstairs walls. He finished several small wiring jobs, finally connected the front doorbell, oiled some rusting doorknob innards, and plugged a squirrel hole. He replaced a pressure control valve he'd been having doubts about for years, and renewed every faucet washer. He finished caulking the chimney, adjusted its hat, and spray-painted its surrounding flashing. He sealed and painted the front steps.

He set himself a deadline—something he'd never done before—and as the date approached, worked longer and longer hours to meet it.

I don't know whether he met his deadline in the end, but if he missed it, it wasn't by much. I found him standing on the lawn outside, gazing at the house in an almost trance-like state. "There it is," he said hoarsely, gesturing toward it with satisfaction. His voice was always hoarse when he was exhausted. "I would have put another coat on the fascia boards, but they don't really look like they need it yet. What do you think?"

The question startled me. I couldn't remember him ever asking me what I thought about anything.

"No, I don't think they need it yet," I said after a moment, trying to sound knowledgeable enough to make it stick. "They look good for another three or four years to me."

He looked dubious, but apparently agreed.

The next day I drove Father down to the lawyer's office, where the final papers were to be signed. Father was a bit disappointed not to see the buyer there, because he'd envisioned a ceremonial handing over of the keys, a formal gesture of some kind. "I want for his hand to shake," he tried to explain to the English lawyer. "Say him *willkommen*; wish for him good. It be, how you say Peter? *wichtig*, yes, important, very much."

The lawyer thought this notion charming, but explained that the buyer was at this moment in a meeting in the offices of his lawyer, signing the same papers, which would be faxed over later that afternoon. "That's how we do things in Canada," he shrugged, gathering up all the papers. "I see your point, but that's not how we do it here."

On the way home—which would be at Heidi's place now, until Father's apartment was ready—we pulled over in front of the house for a final look. The bush beneath my old bedroom—the one Carle Anderson had hidden behind years ago—was in full bloom, and the new stucco set off nicely against the rust-red roof. The front door looked newly painted, and the eaves troughs had new down-pipes. I saw that Father had even re-cemented the old walkway between our front stairs and the street.

I was experiencing sharply mixed feelings, the way I always did about the past, but I don't think Father was. "They've got three kids, just like we did," he mused, sucking vigorously on his teeth, something he'd been doing increasingly in recent years. "I'm glad that breakfast nook will finally get used. I always felt bad about it being wasted."

"How old are their kids?"

"He didn't say. But they'll be able to raise rabbits and

vegetables and geraniums just like you kids did. It'll be good to see that back yard used again."

"I don't think many kids do those sorts of things anymore, Father."

"Of course they do," Father said. "Kids are kids, no matter where you go."

Two weeks later, when I passed by on my way to Fraser Street, I was stunned to discover that the house was gone.

I slammed to a stop and pulled the car off the street and against the curb.

It really had vanished. Simply disappeared.

All that remained were fresh bulldozer tracks crisscrossing an expanse of black, neatly levelled dirt.

TOCCATA IN 'D'

one

April, 1943

The sexton's house at 2657 Kirchallee stood next to the town's only bus stop, so the sexton would have seen Margarete Klassen through his living room window as soon as she stepped off the bus.

A tall young woman, blonde, too young, and probably not plain enough to slip into her new position entirely unnoticed.

That, I suspect, would have annoyed him. He'd always been a traditionalist, and this cursed war was making a shambles of even the most venerable traditions. Even the organists were becoming younger and younger, and changing positions with an almost indecent nonchalance. The last one, who'd insisted on being called von Berlingen on the strength of some bit of ribbon old Bismarck was said to have pinned on her grandfather, hadn't lasted more than two years. And every time the church door opened with their arrival or departure, letting in great gusts of secular wind, it took him longer and longer to put things back into their proper place.

This one wouldn't have looked any different. Those thick, luxurious braids encircling her anxious, eager face spelled trouble, he'd have known that in his bones, and been irritated to realize there was nothing he could do about it, nothing he could do to stop her, nothing for it but to watch her carry her suitcases up the front yard steps and ring the harness bells over the door, and to let her in.

What he wouldn't have given for another organist like old Bachmann. He'd said *Gruess Gott* when he'd arrived at age thirty, and *Vergelt's Gott* when he'd left the post twenty years later, and hardly a word in between.

two

January, 1971

We found the sexton's house still standing, and still inhabited, but nobody answered when my Onkel Hans-Egon knocked. We followed a narrow flagstone path from the house to the nearby church, but it was also empty. I walked around the church and then the house in silence, not quite sure how I felt about them, or whether they meant anything to me at all.

The church must have doubled as a small fortress in medieval times. Its thick-walled Romanesque bell tower was vented on three sides by small slit-windows, and its dome was sheathed in heavy copper. A latticework of iron bars covered its larger nave windows. Nothing from the outside hinted at its lavish baroque interior, which I'd seen in photographs my mother had shown me of the five years she'd served here as the church organist.

The sexton's house was built of the same quarried stone as the church. It was a modest cottage, with inlaid decorative tile and a scalloped roof. The twin dormers under the gable, marking the room where I'd been born, were right where she'd told me they would be. Both the house and the church and even the nearby graveyard were so well kept and so orderly, it made me feel almost sad, even a little irritated, that so much of our history, all that love and anger, all those misunderstandings, anxieties and dreams, could have burned and danced in this place leaving so little outward sign of the struggle.

It began to dawn on me why it might be simpler and easier to know, or to find, one's history irretrievably eradicated.

three

The *Notice of Position Vacant* on the bulletin board at the Johannesstift School of Music in Berlin, 1943, hadn't provoked much interest. Wallenstein was only a country hamlet in the backwoods of Midwestern Germany, where the people were clannish and there was little to do. But for Margarete Klassen, the posting had smelled of escape, and she'd applied immediately. According to her music teacher, whom I tracked down thirty years later, she'd been the only applicant.

Margarete Klassen had an unbridled love for music. She played the pipe organ with a passion, as well as flute, piano, harpsichord and recorder. She composed instrumental music, songs, librettos and poetry, and directed choral groups whenever she could get the chance. Her devout Mennonite parents sometimes worried whether so much artistic fervour could coexist with a true dedication to Reformation principles, but she'd begged and pleaded, and finally convinced them to let her study both music and nursing in Berlin. “Music may be my passion,” she’d assured her father, patriarch of a seventeen-member family and Elder of the Blumenthal Mennonite Church, “but God’s will is my mainstay.” That may have sounded a bit too self-assured coming from a young girl who’d never been on her own before, but her father had apparently suppressed his doubts.

The Wallenstein posting—to a Lutheran church—was available immediately. Margarete packed her bags that same day, swore her roommate Rosalinde to secrecy, and convinced her perplexed school principal not to tell anyone where she was going. She said she’d contact her parents herself. So when the Berlin advocate, whom no one has ever seen fit to name, showed up at the school for another “visit,” Margarete was gone, and Rosalinde made no effort to hide her triumph. Maybe now he’d consider spending a bit more time with his wife and children, she said.

The man was so astonished, he seemed to miss the jab entirely.

Where on earth had she gone? Was there no message? No forwarding address?

Especially not that, Rosalinde assured him grimly.

Then she couldn’t resist giving him a very forthright piece of her mind. He was a sneak and a scoundrel, she said, no matter how much Margarete may have fallen for him. If she hadn’t come to her senses, he’d have pursued her until she was utterly compromised—Rosalinde had no doubts about that. If he had any decency at all, which she doubted, he would now head for the nearest church and get down on his knees, begging forgiveness of the ever-merciful Lord. There was, after all, the example of the publican Zaccheus . . .

But Rosalinde was preaching down an empty stairway. The jurist had turned and fled.

four

The sexton's house had been divided into two apartments—one for the sexton, the other for the organist. But since the sexton had a wife and three teenage sons, he'd found this arrangement quite unfair, and made no bones about it to the Reverend Markengraf. His other complaint concerned the young organist's playing style, which he found 'un-Christian'. "When she's not pacing through the graveyard as if the Devil were on her back, she's in there hour after hour, playing as if she were the Devil herself!" he groused one Sunday afternoon, after an unsuccessful attempt at a nap.

The Reverend Markengraf, who'd been standing on the flagstone path listening to the resonating pipes, might have agreed, but the sexton's constant complaints were becoming tiresome. "You exaggerate immoderately, Herr Krueger. As always." But he ambled over to the church and let himself in at the sacristy door, to wait for her at the baptismal font until she was through.

The music from the choir loft was tossing and seething about the vaulted ceiling like a midsummer storm. Gust after gust of ascendant scales spiralled up the keyboard, the triads more and more shrill as the dissonances rose in the updraft and began to dominate. Pipe blasts skirled, piercing and thin, the notes coiling, flaring, spinning and whirling, up, up, more and more breathless, ever more desperate, higher and higher, straining toward the edge, the very rim's outer edge—then a rending flash, like shattering glass—and the chords fell back through the heavy air, tumbling, plunging, swiftly gathering, darkening, until with an abrupt roar they burst into huge melodic thunder, long sonorous torrents of rich, booming harmonics that resounded to the very base of the skull and saturated every pore of the body.

It was an utterly unapologetic Bach showpiece, a frenzied celebration of tumult and turmoil, and the Reverend Markengraf found himself glancing apprehensively at the old familiar pipes in spite of himself, though it wasn't the solid, two hundred-year-old instrument he was worried about.

Eventually the final chords boiled up from the bottom of the keyboard, feigned an ending in the obligatory Baroque manner, and then the trumpets brayed the finale, a massive drawn-out major signature so vast and all-encompassing, it drowned out everything in its path, burying fear, confusion, pain, and even thought itself. The organist leaned on the keys until the billowing thunder reverberated to the very stone foundations of the little church itself—and then the music ceased, and drained away.

The Reverend heard the clap of the keyboard cover, and then she was coming down the aisle, a furtive, diminutive figure with a sheaf of sheet music in her hand, her bowed head barely distinguishable through the gloom.

He waited until she had reached the last pew, then cleared his throat. "Fraülein Klassen, that sort of music . . ." But at the sight of her abruptly raised eyes, still blazing with the turbulence of the toccata, he stopped short and simply muttered, "Such a . . . fervent . . . playing style, Fraülein Klassen, it might strike some as . . . as somewhat inappropriate for a quiet country church."

Margarete drew herself up to her full height, spun around and confronted the Reverend with reckless abruptness. "The Toccata in D, Pastor Markengraf," she snapped, her voice almost cracking with emotion, "The Toccata in D must be played so that it hits one like a walking stick whacked across the back!"

Both startled, they stared at each other in mutual astonishment, then Margarete blushed furiously and fled.

five

Throughout most of the war, Reinhard Niebuhr had carried a scrap of paper in his wallet on which he'd written *2657 Kirchallee, Wallenstein*. When his best friend Gerhard had first managed to tease this address out of one of Margarete's sisters, Reinhard had written it in pencil, but had since redrawn it many times in ink. He'd done this despite Gerhard's frank opinion that he was simply wasting his time. Whatever Margarete's plans might be, they didn't seem to include Reinhard.

Even if his friend was right, Reinhard refused to give up hope. It might have been true in the past, but the situation was constantly changing. Reinhard had grown up in West Prussia not far from the Klassen farm, and had fallen in love with the spirited Margarete the moment he'd caught sight of her at a summer Bible camp. The two couldn't have been more unalike—she, a gregarious, passionate lover of music and literature; he, a loner, an introvert with a penchant for technical drafting and scientific photography and really no interest in the arts at all.

But for Reinhard that had been the very source of the attraction. From his solitary corner at parties and church meetings he'd watched "his Margarete," surrounded by friends or bobbing from group to group, playing piano or conducting the Youth Choir, directing biblical plays or skits of her own invention at weddings, Young People's meetings, church benefits—watched her hungrily, longing for that same ability to mingle, to express himself, to release himself from his own rib-cage. Or, failing that, at least to share that spirit by association: to win her for a wife.

God only knows how he'd gotten up the nerve to propose to her. Even Gerhard had advised against it. But he'd persisted, he'd proposed—and she'd turned him down. Only she'd been awfully nice about it, said she was flattered but that she simply wasn't thinking about marriage just yet, that she had many other plans—and he in turn had heard himself blurting, just before he'd escaped, that that was alright, that he could wait, it didn't matter how long. And later on, in his own somewhat blurred recollection of the incident, this promise had come to constitute for him the grounds for further hope.

So he'd taken her image back into his solitary corner and settled down to wait. And while he waited, he worked. He was a good craftsman, a compulsive perfectionist, and under the constant rub and polish of his thoughts she grew more extraordinary with every year that passed, more pure, ever saintlier, until she shone like an icon or beacon and illuminated his entire life.

In January 1943 at the Russian front, as his unit lay surrounded under murderous crossfire by the Red Army troops of Stalingrad, he wrote to her in Berlin: I don't know if God will lead me out of this Valley of the Shadow of Death, but if He does, I will come to see you. His letter arrived three weeks after he did, and she was completely disoriented by his visit. She stammered that she really didn't . . . well, she just simply hadn't . . . no, she hadn't received any letter, and besides . . . oh Lord, it was all so confusing. She just didn't know what to do. No, no, she didn't want to talk about marriage, heavens no, least of all that. At the puzzled, half-hurt look that spread across his face she hastened to assure him that it wasn't him . . . it wasn't . . . well not exactly . . . in fact . . . well not at all, not at all. It was all just . . . at which point she burst into tears and he fled once more, uneasy and perplexed, and with a growing, unnamable fear gnawing at his insides.

But he dealt with this as he had always dealt with such fears. He brought down one of the big steel doors, of which he had many inside him, and sectioned it off. And since no resolution had been reached, he went on waiting. Eventually the army ordered him back to Warsaw, where the Poles were fighting an increasingly effective partisan war. He was a pacifist by faith and nature, so they made him a cook.

six

Since we couldn't find anyone at home, Hans-Egon decided to document our visit with some commemorative photographs. But he'd no sooner climbed into the garden of an adjacent house for better focal length, when the door behind him snapped open, and an old woman, with broomsticks waving in her eyes, demanded to know just what the devil he was doing in her petunias.

Caught red-handed, Hans-Egon apologized profusely, agreed entirely that climbing into someone's garden without permission was indeed an outrage, that at the very least he might have knocked on her door to ask, and that yes, yes, without question, this was yet another example of the Americanization of German morals.

When she had calmed down a bit, Hans-Egon went on to explain that he had driven down from Hamburg that morning with his young nephew here, a writer over on a short visit from Canada, who'd been born twenty-five years ago in the sexton's house next door, and whom he'd only wished to gratify with a few photographs of the place of his birth.

At that, the old lady became quite fascinated with us. She stared at me intently through her wire-rimmed glasses and then announced that indeed, yes indeed, she believed she remembered this young man; she remembered him lying in a baby buggy on the church path. He would have been only a month or two old at the time, if memory served. My my, how extraordinary, how very extraordinary. And a writer did we say? My my, how extraordinary.

"Oldest son of the church organist at the time. You probably remember her as Margarete Klassen," Hans-Egon explained.

"Oh, yes, yes indeed, I remember her quite well. Came here very young, very blonde, very energetic. Seems to me she even led the Young People's choir for a while."

"That was her, unquestionably," Hans-Egon confirmed. "She was my sister. I visited her several times during her time in Wallenstein."

"Oh, did you really? That was good of you, I'm sure. Yes, yes, she would have enjoyed that, being all alone in those days, at least at the beginning, at the very beginning, before her entire family . . ." The old lady's memory seemed to have encountered dangerous ground; her eyes hooded briefly while she searched for a way out. "I mean to say, those were difficult times, of course; difficult times."

"You're referring to the Great Trek of 1945," Hans-Egon commiserated, though his voice had taken on a slight edge. "Yes, that must have come as a shock for you, being inundated by so many refugees. But at least you still had your farms..."

"An invasion, an absolute invasion!" the old lady agreed. "Wagons upon wagons of them, and so many women and children. And the horses! My God, we hadn't seen so many horses since the army took away all of ours for the last offensive."

"My family fled over five hundred kilometres from West Prussia to the West," Hans-Egon pointed out. "They had to abandon everything they owned. People who died along the way couldn't even be properly buried. Half the time the Trek wasn't more than a few hours ahead of the Russian tanks."

"That's why those poor horses were so neglected, of course," the old lady agreed. "Yes, yes, I suppose one shouldn't judge."

Hans-Egon sighed, swung his camera over his shoulder, and paused for a moment to scrutinize the sky. "*Mit Verlaub,*" he said, and I thought his voice became a shade less polite than custom demanded. "You will excuse me, *gnaedige Frau*, but if it came to a question of judgment, I'd treat that subject with a certain caution. The citizens of Wallenstein, you will recall, didn't retain an entirely unblemished reputation . . ."

"Unusual times," the old lady bridled before I could ask for an explanation. "Unusual times, unusual circumstances."

"Unusual indeed," Hans-Egon agreed. "We hadn't often seen houses with a toilet bolted down in the middle of every room in the house. Including the kitchen!"

He turned to me with a slightly sour smirk, ignoring

the darkening face of the old woman. “After the war, you see, those who’d been spared the bombs were obliged to share their extra rooms with those who’d been bombed out. Only one’s bathrooms were exempt.”

“They came in here by the thousands,” the old woman muttered defensively. “By the tens of thousands. Acting as though we owed them a living.”

Hans-Egon glanced at his watch, then turned to the garden gate. “I expect we should be off; we’ve taken far too much of your valuable time already,” he observed. “Very nice to have met you though.” And as we started down the garden path: “Oh, one last question if I may—is the old Reverend Markengraf still alive by any chance?”

“The Canon Markengraf,” the old woman corrected icily, “is still very much among the living. He resides on Lanzer Street, five doors from the end.”

And then she slammed the door.

seven

June, 1944

The sexton's house seemed deserted the morning Reinhard Niebuhr climbed down off the army truck, thanked the driver for the ride, and rang the harness bells above the door. Nothing stirred, and after repeated janglings he stood motionless for a moment, staring irresolutely at the unblinking dormer windows above his head.

Then he heard the sound of the organ pipes drifting faintly across the little graveyard through the chestnut trees. The postern gate was open, and so was the church's sacristy door. He slipped in, set down his kit bag on the umbrella stand, and stopped by the side of the baptismal font, waiting for his eyes to adjust to the dark. His heart was pounding like a kettle drum.

The music coming through the gloom seemed muted, distant. After a few moments he could make out the curve of her back, bending lightly over the keyboard, the top of her head faintly haloed by the tiny reading lamp above the score. He stood there for what must have been half an hour at least, hardly noticing the passing time, hardly hearing the faraway music. The gong in the bell tower bonged the quarter hour.

And then he saw her coming down the stairs, and he cleared his throat so she wouldn't be frightened. She stopped at the first pew and squinted a little; he'd forgotten those rimless spectacles she'd begun to wear at the music school in Berlin.

"Is that you, Reinhard?"

"Yes . . . I've . . . I got a few days furlough. And I found a ride."

They gazed at each other for a long time, and then she sat down in the pew, her face shadowed by the font.

"And what brings you to Wallenstein, Reinhard?"

The suddenness of the question startled him, though he'd been asking himself the same thing for the past three days now, trying to find transport from one devastated city to another, crossing five hundred kilometres of bombed and torn-up countryside from Danzig to the heavily fortified west bank of the Oker River.

"It's really an awful mess out there," he said wonderingly.

She said nothing for some moments, then nodded slowly. "The Allied bombers fly over day and night."

"Even little Blumenthal's been destroyed."

From behind the choir loft, the organ bellows in the bell tower wheezed and sighed away the last remaining air.

He was thinking that she'd probably never marry him. He was also thinking that she might. And the two thoughts were quite unrelated because he was totally convinced of both and had never felt it possible to reconcile the paradox. She was so far out of his range, with her music, her popularity, her reading and teaching. And he didn't know why it simply had to be this girl, but it did.

"I've come again to ask you to marry me," he said. "Unless it's still too soon, in which case . . ."

She looked at him slowly, without expression. "In which case, what, Reinhard?"

He felt very aware of his awkwardness, his unease—but no less certain for all that. "In which case I'll come back again, later, maybe in a year or so?" he said.

She said nothing for a long time. He watched the shadowy outline of her bowed head, until he realized from its faintly rhythmic movements that she was crying.

He didn't know what to do about that, so he just stood by the font and waited, loving her very much, feeling helpless.

After a long time she dug into her dress pocket for a handkerchief, blew into it, dried her eyes and cheeks and put it back.

"When I was in Berlin," she said hesitantly. "When I was in Berlin, I fell in love with a man who . . . was married. I came here to . . . get away from all that . . ."

He felt himself tensing, apprehensive.

"I . . . I just can't give you an answer now, Reinhard. I just don't know what I want, or what I should do. I seem to want so many . . . contradictory things." She saw his anxiety and reached for his hand impulsively, stroking it as if it was a small frightened animal. "Oh I know I'm being hard on you, Reinhard, and I feel badly about it, but you've got to understand this from my side too. I keep feeling completely smothered, as if every time I come up there's another wave pushing me down again, and I just can't seem to get any air!"

He nodded numbly, protected by her gently stroking fingers, her warmth, her caring. He'd never been touched like that by a woman before.

"How many days of furlough do you have left?"

He had been given two weeks' leave, and it had taken him four days to reach Wallenstein. And no, he had no other relatives or friends in the West; everyone he knew was in Prussia.

"Then why don't you stay with us and rest for a few days? The Pastor has a guest room in his attic; I'm sure he'd put you up. And Hans-Egon's coming for a visit the day after tomorrow; maybe the three of us could do some hiking in Braunschweig."

He agreed without even thinking about it. And for the next five days he stood at the window of the Pastor's attic guest room, staring fixedly across the road toward the sexton's house and Margarete's curtained bedroom window, burning its image into his memory as if by doing so he might somehow be able to draw her into his life by the sheer force of his longing.

On the sixth day of his visit he managed to find a camera and some chemicals, and spent the entire day on the lawn and in the Pastor's kitchen, developing and printing a remarkably sharp and detailed photograph of the little cottage and its dormer window. The photograph was so intense, and made the cottage seem so prominent and imposing, that Margarete found herself blushing uneasily every time she looked at it.

Reinhard gave it to her as a present on the day he left.

eight

Lanzer Street was only half a dozen blocks from the sexton's house, and we found the Markengraf residence quite easily. The old man was indeed very much alive; in fact, he was irrepressible, and he remembered Hans-Egon immediately "despite the absence of that splendid officer's uniform you always wore. And this young man" (he took a step closer and appraised me with a sharp look), "unless I miss my guess, must be the oldest son of our dear departed Margarete Niebuhr—have I got it right?"

I was so astonished I almost forgot to shake his hand, and he seemed hugely pleased. "Ha ha, that surprised you a little, did it? *Ja* well, you see I've always had an unusual gift for remembering faces, and your mouth and nose recall your mother's to a turn. But please, come in, come in; I'm keeping you standing in the cold."

"Well I must say, this is all very exciting—to receive a visit from Kanada, from the same young man I christened in the sexton's house nearly twenty-five years ago! Who would have predicted it? Please, have a seat on the sofa, my niece will bring us coffee, and then you must tell us all the news. Heaven knows after so many years there must be plenty."

He let himself fall comfortably into an armchair and beamed at us across the table, a burly, fit-looking man in his seventies, with plenty of graying hair and not a trace of clerical pomposity.

"Now let me see: you left for Kanada in 1951 in one of those condemned old grain freighters your Canadian Railway Company bought from the scrap yards in Bremerhaven. Have I got that right?" He seemed to thrive like a schoolboy on the guessing-game approach. "To be honest, our town administrator told me this because he had to sign the papers. And then—oh Liesl, have you put on the coffee?—we'll have that coffee in just a few minutes. Yes, and then you journeyed to British Kolumbia, but more than this I do not know. Aside from the death of your mother, of course, which was a great blow."

While I entertained the old Canon with descriptions of the last-minute confusions and bunglings that had bedevilled our emigration from the Port of Bremen, Frau Markengraf, a kindly, twinkle-eyed little potato of a woman, took the opportunity to scrutinize me carefully over the lowered rims of her bifocals. "And your lady mother," she said eventually, giving the impression of great circumspection. "Was she content, in Kanada?"

She watched me wrestle with the question, and then nodded gently. "Your mother and I were very close, you see. We often spent whole afternoons together, sewing and talking about all sorts of things . . ."

"My parents shipped over to Canada as indentured servants," I said. "A fairly common arrangement, I'm told. Farmers in Canada paid the fare in advance, then worked the immigrants till the debt was repaid. My parents hoed corn and beans by hand for almost two years to repay our sixty dollar passage."

Frau Markengraf shook her head sadly. "*Mein Gott,* her fingers must have been ruined."

"Well, there wasn't an organ around anyway, as far as I know. I think the nearest one was more than a hundred kilometres away. In a Catholic church."

The coffee arrived, and Frau Markengraf passed around a tray of fresh pound cake and lemon tarts.

"You know," old Markengraf mused after some moments, "they left for Kanada awfully hastily, I always thought. I often wondered why. Your father, after all, had secured a cabinet-making apprenticeship just a few kilometers away, and your mother could have stayed with us indefinitely. She was a superb musician—the best we ever had. I always thought we'd lose her some day to some cathedral, in Marienburg, say, or in Köln."

I pushed back my coffee cup and wiped my mouth with the stiff linen serviette. "Actually, there are a number of things that have never really added up for me. Unfortunately my mother died when I was barely nineteen, and most of the questions I should have asked her then are only occurring to me now."

I refolded the serviette and settled back into the cushions. "Like why she and my father ever married, for example. That's been puzzling me for years. The more I try to understand it, the more unlikely the match becomes."

Hans-Egon sighed and swirled the coffee in his cup.

"You said you used to spend a lot of time with my mother, Frau Markengraf. Perhaps you gained some insight into her thinking at the time?"

The good lady seemed less surprised by the question than concerned about its propriety.

"Your honorable father," she said gently, tracing a careful circle on the tablecloth with her fingernail, "Your honorable father was a very good man. He worked exceedingly hard. He was modest, and thoroughly honest. And he loved your mother very much."

I leaned forward slightly to acknowledge the tribute. "Yes, I know that's true. My father adored my mother, and she always treated him with respect and affection." Frau Markengraf looked relieved. "But nevertheless, I can't help feeling that their marriage was a total mismatch. It spelled the end of my mother's career in music, and also my father's as a cabinet-maker. And it landed them both in a country where they remained strangers all their lives. Yet whatever they had between them didn't seem to make up the difference, as far as I could see."

"Yes, but that's something people don't value enough nowadays," old Markengraf intoned, and for the first time I caught a hint of the clerical echo. "When a person believes in something bigger than himself—or herself, as the case may be—she can be capable of extraordinary feats of faith. Your mother was a deep and strong believer, son. A wholly dedicated Christian woman. Once she had given her promise in holy matrimony, she kept that promise, whether or not it happened to . . ."

"But that still doesn't . . ." I interrupted, then stopped because Frau Markengraf had cleared her throat and glanced at her husband in mild reproach.

"I hope I will not stand accused of betraying confidences," she said, looking down at her hands. "Your mother did not have an easy life."

She hesitated, searching for the appropriate words. "Your mother, God rest her soul, always had a very . . . how shall I put it . . . somewhat ambivalent luck when it came to romance. She very desperately wanted to marry someone with whom she could share her enthusiasm for music and literature, but that was considered among your people as rather self-indulgent. And to make things worse, for some strange reason every man who courted her turned out to be more interested in physics, or medicine—anything but music. Of course there was (as her husband looked ready to interrupt), well yes, there was one exception, a young arts administrator, or maybe he was an advocate, from—do you remember, Paul? from Berlin, I think, or thereabouts, with whom your mother had fallen in love—but that was before she came to Wallenstein, and he was a married man in any case. He even followed her here, now that I think of it, although that was already after she'd married your father—he was interned at the time, as a prisoner of war . . . yes, came for a visit all the way from Berlin, this advocate, but of course your mother sent him away.

"In any case, as I was saying, her suitors all seemed to have been . . . inappropriate, one after another, and then there was your father, a good, decent man, who had asked for her hand repeatedly over the years . . ." She sighed again, and shrugged. "Well, you can imagine how it was, with the war everywhere, and all the uncertainty . . . "

She looked at me directly then and nodded. "Yes, yes, you're quite right of course, and she also had many doubts about the wisdom of that union. But, in the end . . ."

"Nevertheless, the salt of the earth," old Markengraf insisted. "More quiet than most, not given to a lot of socializing, and he could be a bit uncompromising at times, I'll give you that. I remember the time the sexton hit him, during an argument over your father's share of the well water—I believe old Krueger was trying to appropriate it for his goats. In any case, your father took that blow to court, and didn't let go until the man was finally fined—despite the fact that the case took over eight months, and he had to travel all the way to Hanover several times to make it stick. When he saw his rights infringed he was relentless, I won't say otherwise. But, but, he treated your mother like a saint, and he was an upright Christian. He used to plough my garden for me, and never expected anything in return. One shouldn't underestimate such qualities, even if they do seem to be unfashionable nowadays."

He reached energetically for the swan-necked coffee pot and poured, filling his cup in a single swirl precisely to that imaginary line, two-thirds of the way up the side, that my mother had always said was a sure sign of refinement and breeding.

"But all this still doesn't explain to me why they felt

it necessary to give up a promising future in Braunschweig, to set out like refugees for the wilds of Kanada . . ."

As we sat and talked through the afternoon, I glanced occasionally around the room and out into the garden, at the rows of marigolds forming a perfect H-pattern from the house to the alley, and the meticulously weeded half-moons of scarlet sage, set like plucked eyebrows above their fieldstone borders. The house, too, was trim and immaculate, with walls and floors so neatly cut and finished, there'd been no need for mouldings anywhere that I could see.

And I remembered how my father used to stare about him in the living rooms of the Canadian houses in which we'd lived, his brow creased with despair, his mouth tight with disdain, and in his hands his ever-present measuring tape.

My father had carried that tape about him the way most men carry a pocket watch, and he'd consulted it just as regularly. He would stare at a door jamb or window frame with the brooding look of a confirmed doomsayer, then leap up, make a few swift measurements, and sit back down again, disgusted. He'd always owned two tapes, as I recalled—a wide, chrome-plated Lufkin for the six workdays of the week, and a little black one, small enough to fit inconspicuously into the watch-pocket of his only suit, for Sundays.

nine

Father's photograph of the sexton's house survived the voyage to Canada, and became a fixture in our lives for the next two decades. Mother tacked it above the sofa in the two-room shack we inhabited when we first arrived in Canada, and on the living room wall of the tiny bungalow that followed. She hung it over the mantelpiece of the little farmhouse on the twenty-five acre mixed dairy farm in Agassiz we eventually managed to sign for at the bank. It hung above the piano in the house we bought in Vancouver after the farm went bankrupt, and it was under that photograph fiveyears later that I wrestled the kitchen knife out of my father's hand the day our church minister came to tell us that my mother had been killed in a car accident on the highway.

At the news my father went grey as a stone, and then sank to the floor with an animal-like croak, and for the next half hour he just sat there glazed-eyed, unmoving, his mouth working emptily and his fingers spread wide apart like a frog's.

I sent the minister away and then held father's shoulders and tried to rock him, instinctively, blindly, both of us totally in shock. And then he started that terrifying, inhuman moaning, thrashing and flinging himself about the floor, crashing heedlessly into tables and chairs and crying out again and again: "My fault! My fault! My fault!"

That made no sense and I told him so, but I doubt that he even heard. Eventually he slowed a little and then stopped and laid still, a curled-up ball under the dining room table, and I hoped he might sleep a while so I covered him with a blanket. But a few minutes later I heard another low moan and came running just in time to see him, staggering and wild-eyed, with the knife in his fist. Fortunately he was still quite weak and I took it from him easily. Then I managed to get him to bed.

That night, when I finally got to bed myself, I heard him crying and praying in his room across the hall, and when I woke up several hours later, and then again several hours after that, he was still crying and praying desperately, like a drowning man. I had never in my life heard a grown man cry, and the sound of it was so unnatural and so inexpressibly awful, I kept having to fight down the impulse to throw up. The next night was the same, and after the third I simply couldn't take it any more. I bent apart the blades of an old fan until it clattered loudly enough to drown him out. From that night on I plugged it in as soon as he began to cry.

ten

At the little restaurant *Zum Goldenen Hirsch,* which old Markengraf had assured us was still in business, Hans-Egon and I hung up our hats and coats and sat down at one of its few tables.

"Your mother used to drop in here quite regularly," Hans-Egon recalled, scrutinizing the interior with a mixture of fondness and regret. "I believe she used to pick up her daily order of milk from this place."

The walls were decorated with stuffed deer trophies and old breechloaders, and the coat-hooks were bits of antler screwed to the posts and beams. The proprietress wore a bulky sweater under her floor-length apron, and there was no menu.

"The restaurant simply serves whatever the family is having for supper," Hans-Egon explained. "She just cooks extra portions for the trade."

I found that charming—in fact, I found the entire village charming. Hans-Egon was more cynical. "Don't be fooled by the décor; they can be a hard-hearted bunch when the going gets tough," he shrugged. "Right now everyone's comfortably off and the future looks good. Back in '45 they treated the refugees like dirt, and your mother's parents too. Old Markengraf refused to give Bibles to the refugees, though he had stacks of them in his church. That infuriated your mother, as you might imagine."

"You're kidding. The Canon Markengraf? That easy-going, hospitable old man?"

"Well he wasn't so easy-going back then. Didn't your mother ever tell you about the buttons? He used to drop a handful of big overcoat buttons into the collection bag every Sunday, which your mother had to fish out after every sermon and return to him after church. I believe they had themselves quite an altercation over that, eventually.

"But that aside, they did get along fairly well, all things considered. The old man wasn't really fibbing about that. And I think your mother was quite well accepted in the town. It wasn't until we all came pouring in from the east that things became . . . complicated. I think if your parents had stayed, somebody would eventually have moved over and given them some room. You might have become an academic, or a cleric, or a white-collar quill-driver of some kind. I don't think you even have to believe in God to be a cleric these days."

I laughed. "No, no, Hans-Egon, I'll admit the notion that I might have grown up German makes me flinch, but not because I may have narrowly missed a triumphant career in hymn-writing. To be honest, ever since I've arrived in this country I've found myself walking around it in a sort of mental half-crouch, trying not to shake too much dust off that part of me that instinctively fits into place here. It's a part I've never much liked, and have always had to fight very hard to suppress. I'm already inclined to be self-righteous enough as it is; you set me into an environment that actually fosters such characteristics, and I'd have grown into a raving pedant.

"You think I'm being unfair? I took a walk this morning, out to the Althauser Wald, and where the trail enters the forest I saw a neatly printed official sign that read: *BRISK WALK THROUGH THIS FOREST: 150 CALORIES.* Now that's bad enough. What's worse is that when I first saw the sign, I simply thought it impressive. You know—thorough. I did."

We laughed ruefully, and I signalled to the proprietress for a second round and more *Wuerstchen.*

"No, seriously though; every time I take a trip out of my huge, empty country, I come back feeling downright grateful that we didn't end up anywhere else. I even get the odd twinge of guilt that it was bought at such a price—our parents laying their lives into the muck so we could cross over on dry feet. It still makes me feel uncomfortable whenever I think about it. I don't like to be that beholden to anyone—not even to parents."

Hans-Egon nodded thoughtfully. "They really were a mess, those first ten years, weren't they?"

"A mess? Lord, you have no idea. I can still see my mother, who was terrified stiff of anything larger than a bird, trying to milk six cows by hand on our farm in

Agassiz. And when the money ran out, my father took a job at a local hotel washing pots and pans on the night shift—he had to milk our cows at noon and at midnight to fit everything in. To which the cows didn't respond with great enthusiasm. Nor the family, I have to admit.

"Then finally, after fifteen years of working like slaves to repay a $10,000 debt and the interest, just when they expected they'd be able to breathe just a little easier and live like human beings again, the sky caved in and Father lost the only reason he ever had for breathing. Worse even than that, he seemed to think it was his own fault."

"His fault?"

"I know, it sounds absurd, and I tried to tell him that, but I just couldn't get through to him at the time. Actually, I never have figured out what he was talking about. He just kept crying my fault! my fault! that afternoon when we got the news, and then (I lowered my voice instinctively)—I've never told this to anyone, Hans-Egon; please keep this strictly to yourself—then he tried to kill himself with a kitchen knife, and after that, for more than the next half year, he prayed in his bedroom every night like a . . . well, like a man on the edge of . . . damnation."

As I'd talked, Hans-Egon had become very agitated. At the description of my father's praying he looked almost ill. He passed a dejected hand over his forehead and pushed his beer away. "Oh my God," he sighed, more to himself than to me. "My God, what a mess."

He pulled a napkin out of the napkin rack and began twisting it absently through his fingers, shredding it into long, irregular pieces. “You know, I suspected something like this. But I didn’t know it had gone that far. I wasn’t . . . Hildegard didn’t tell me about that part of it . . .”

I was perplexed. “Who told you what, Hans-Egon?”

He ran his hands through his hair several times, saying nothing. Then he looked at me directly. “Because he was, you see. That was exactly what he was.”

“What are you talking about?”

He seemed to be reacting to a lot more than I had just told him.

“What’s this about, Hans-Egon? I’ve never told anyone about father’s suicide attempt before. What could you possibly know that I haven’t already . . .”

Hans-Egon just kept shaking his head in mute dismay. I decided to wait.

After a long while, during which he seemed to be collecting his thoughts, Hans-Egon pulled back his mug of beer from between the salt and pepper shakers and went to work trying to position it with absolute precision on the intersection of two deep scratches on the table top.

“You see, I loved your mother very deeply,” he said to the half-filled mug, moving it this way and that without looking up. “She was my sister, but more important to me, she was my friend and closest confidante. And I was hers, which is why I feel some responsibility in all this. I should have known. It was there in the poems she included with her letters, I can see that now, but I guess we’d been apart too long to hear each other very clearly anymore.”

He paused for a moment, while he made another slight correction to the mug's position. "She was a passionate romantic, you see, but the family and the church and the times and, who knows, maybe even she herself, all seemed hell bent to line her wings with stones. There was always talk of duty, of honour, of faith and obedience; never joy or risk or self-expression. So when she fell so deeply in love with that married advocate in Berlin, it was like an otherworldly experience for her—ecstatic, delirious, but also profoundly terrifying and culpable.

"They thought her relationship with this advocate mercifully platonic—but that wasn't true. That is, it was true in Berlin, but as you heard from Frau Markengraf this afternoon, he eventually discovered where she'd flown and followed her here to Wallenstein.

"It was only for a day. Your father was interned as a prisoner of war and she was already pregnant with you, so she didn't even want to let the advocate in the door, but, well, men have their ways of breaking down women's resolve, and in the end he stayed, and the inevitable happened. And I suppose it sounds appalling of me to say it, but I hope for that one night at least she managed to break free."

He looked at me earnestly for a long moment. "I see that this doesn't seem to bother you, and I'm relieved, but those were different times and a different generation, and we couldn't just shrug such things off like you.

"Your mother became so overwhelmed by her guilt, she decided there was nothing for it but to confess it all to your father—a move I fiercely opposed because I felt sure that he'd never be able to handle it. Your father loved your mother very much, and he treated her like a saint—which wasn't as wonderful as it may sound, but that's another story—at the same time she was also the only woman he'd ever courted, and his sense of Christian marriage was hopelessly idealistic, very naive. So in the end she only told him that the advocate had appeared, and that she'd sent him packing, and while this near-collision with catastrophe gave your father a decided turn, I believe he was persuaded that the catastrophe had been averted. However they did decide to emigrate to Kanada very soon after your birth, so who knows what anxieties may have been gnawing away in the back of his mind.

"Certainly as far as your mother was concerned, emigration to Kanada amounted mostly to escape and punishment. The former she desperately needed; the latter she was convinced she deserved. That's why she gave up her career without a murmur, and never really tried to resume it over there. She saw the years of working like a plough-horse as a penance—her only hope for absolution was to be a good and dutiful wife to poor Reinhard.

"And that may sound perverse enough, but what was worse: the prescription didn't work. She sent me a poem a year after she'd emigrated, about a snake in the apple bin that kept coiling more and more tightly around her throat. The following autumn—it was the year she almost bled to death during the birth of your sister Gutrun—I received a long letter in which she said: I have to tell him, Hans-Egon, I have to get this off my conscience; I simply can't draw breath while living with this lie anymore.

"I sent her back a stern note telling her not to be foolish, that the God of our fathers and the God she was invoking had a greater capacity for forgiveness than she was giving him credit for—and besides, what the hell was all that faith good for if she found herself incapable of accepting the reprieve it offered? That seemed to draw off some of the poison, for a few years at any rate, but it was obviously not enough, because eventually she did break down and she told him."

He paused, but I didn't look up. I had been trying to reassemble the torn bits of napkin he had pushed into a heap beside the ashtray, but I wasn't having much luck.

Hans-Egon waited until several customers had brushed past our table and the door had muffled the sounds of traffic outside.

"It was the night before she died," he said finally. "The night before she died. Your father confided all this in total desperation to your Aunt Hildegard several days later. According to Hildegard, your mother confessed the whole affair to him that night before she went to bed, and then she got down on her knees and begged him for his forgiveness."

I felt sick. I didn't want to hear any more. I glanced at Hans-Egon and then stared very hard at my hands on the table, which were piling the napkin shreds back against the ashtray. I was trying to figure out how I was going to rid myself of all this. Trying not to have to see that appalling image again. But the question must have shown in my eyes nevertheless.

"The answer is no," Hans-Egon said quietly, bringing his mug to top dead centre on the lines. "She asked for his forgiveness, but he couldn't give it.

"And the next afternoon, she died."

Acknowledgements

Thanks to Sam Steiner, Archivist at the Mennonite Archives of Ontario, for access to the Hunsberger photo collection; and to Hiro Boga and Ron Smith for great cover design and editorial suggestions. They made the process seem effortless.

Reviews of Andreas Schroeder's Books

About the novel *Dustship Glory:*

"A brilliant saga of the dust-bedevilled thirties on the prairies; a powerful portrait of an irascible, heroic man, part prophetic genius, part damaged outcast, and his impossible, magnificent dream."

—Margaret Laurence

"With *Dustship Glory,* his tale of the visionary Tom Sukanen, Andreas Schroeder has joined the sparse and powerful company of writers, made up of Kroetsch, Wiebe and Vanderhaeghe, whose prairie saints and madmen have taken hold and will never let go of this country's imagination. What Schroeder has accomplished is, quite simply, magical."

—Timothy Findley

"*Dustship Glory* is the moving story of an authentic prophet; that is, of a man considered mad and dangerous by the community, yet who lives according to an expanded sense of reality while everyone around him clings desperately to their illusions in the middle of the waste land of dustbowl Saskatchewan."

—Northrop Frye

About the memoir *Shaking It Rough:*

"Andreas Schroeder has written one of the best "prison" books to date . . . a personal meditation that at times approaches lyricism, and an astonishingly fair-minded account of the system."

—Margaret Atwood

Shaking It Rough will shake up more than a few Canadians who labour under all sorts of misconceptions about life in our prisons."

—Farley Mowat

"A haunting evocation of an alternate life. One meets, in this story of doing time, not a criminal but oneself. After reading this book, I am uneasy, going through doors."

—Robert Kroetsch

Andreas Schroeder is the author of twenty books of poetry, fiction, nonfiction, translations, journalism and literary criticism. His books have won or been shortlisted for many awards including the Governor-General's Award, the Sealbooks First Novel Award, the Stephen Leacock Award, the Arthur Ellis Award for Best Non-Fiction and the Red Maple Award. For his literary journalism he was shortlisted for a National Magazine Award, and won the Canadian Association of Journalists' Best Investigative Journalism Award. He received an Honourary Doctorate of Letters from the University College of the Fraser Valley in 2002.

Schroeder currently holds the Rogers Communications Chair in Creative Nonfiction in the University of British Columbia's Creative Writing Program. He lives in Roberts Creek on BC's Sunshine Coast with his wife Sharon Oddie Brown.